Tom felt himself hurtling through empty space. All around him was a weird nonlight. The black hole! The thought crashed in his head. I've gone through the black hole!

Tom stared around, eager to take in as much as he could. He thought he passed a world, but he wasn't sure. It looked as if a giant had wrung it out.

Then, flashing past him was a contorted parody of a human form. Some parts were enormously large, others ridiculously small. Tom had an awful suspicion some organs were inside-out. Was that a giant liver grossly pulsing out there?

Far ahead of him, Tom could just make out a pinpoint of light. He seemed to be rocketing toward it at an incredible speed. What would he find when he reached it? He'd know in a moment.

Tom was spewed out into sudden, blinding brilliance. He felt a sickening wrench and smashed into something.

Then everything went black.

Books in the Tom Swift® Series

#1 THE BLACK DRAGON
#2 THE NEGATIVE ZONE

Available from ARCHWAY Paperbacks

TOM SWIFT 2
THE NEGATIVE ZONE

VICTOR APPLETON

AN ARCHWAY PAPERBACK
Published by POCKET BOOKS

New York   London   Toronto   Sydney   Tokyo   Singapore

AN ARCHWAY PAPERBACK *Original*

An Archway Paperback published by
POCKET BOOKS, a division of Simon & Schuster
1230 Avenue of the Americas, New York, NY 10020

Produced by Byron Preiss Visual Publications, Inc.
Special thanks to Bill McCay

ISBN: 0-671-67824-8

First Archway Paperback printing April 1991

10 9 8 7 6 5 4 3 2 1

TOM SWIFT, AN ARCHWAY PAPERBACK and colophon
are registered trademarks of Simon & Schuster.

Cover art by Carla Sormanti

Printed in the U.S.A.

IL 6+

THE NEGATIVE ZONE

DANGEROUS? NAH. NOT IF YOU DON'T MIND being blown to bits." Tom Swift laughed at his friends as they came down the stairs of the test bunker. "Really, guys, this experiment is as safe as—" The rest of his words were drowned out by the booming sound of foot-thick steel doors clanging shut.

Rick Cantwell looked a little pale under his tan. "We're not worried, Tom. It's just that you haven't told us what you're doing."

"Look, the blast shields between us and the experiment are as strong as the outside doors."

"B-blast shields?" Mandy Coster's big brown eyes got a little bigger as she stared around the underground bunker.

1

"Come on, Mandy. You, too? Don't you believe in the shirt you gave me?" Tom grinned, pointing to the letters stretching across his lean chest—Genius at Work. "How can you get upset about a little thing like blast shields?" His intense blue eyes twinkled with laughter.

Mandy aimed a mock-punch at Tom's blond head. "You nut. I should have realized you were goofing with us."

"Oh, no. We really are using the experiment vault. And we will need the blast doors."

Now Mandy's pretty face went pale under her chestnut hair. "What for?"

Tom's grin slipped a little. "I don't take chances when I'm punching a hole in the universe."

"A hole?" Mandy echoed. "Like sticking a pin in a balloon?"

"Don't expect the universe to disappear with a pop," Tom told her. "But I do hope to create a black hole in there." He pointed to the experiment vault where his equipment was set up.

"A black hole?" Rick's voice had a definite squeak in it. "Those supergravity things in space films? The ones that eat starships and planets?"

"This won't be a planet eater," Tom said. "I hope you won't be disappointed, but I like to start my experiments small. You'd need a microscope to see this sucker—*if* we make one."

He headed into the test vault to check out a long cylinder mounted in one wall. The cylinder had a twin jutting out of the wall opposite. Arm-thick power cables writhed across the floor, leading to both instruments. "This is a laser—a pretty special one. It doesn't just generate a beam of light, it creates a concentrated stream of ions—"

"Like the superlasers the government was developing," Mandy said eagerly. "Now they turn up only in the science-fiction stories I read."

"Well, they may have some more down-to-earth uses, if this works right," Tom said. "The laser beams will smack into each other right *here*." He pointed to a ten-foot-high metal circle with heavy-duty power cables leading into it.

"Tom Swift and his Electric Doughnut," Rick said.

"This is a little more serious than a flying surfboard," Tom told him. "And, I hope, less dangerous." His last invention, the skyboard, had used magnetic levitation to float above the ground. It had also nearly gotten Tom and Rick killed when a rival of Tom's father tried to steal the technology.

"This is a containment field generator, to keep the black hole in its place. It will also hold the starter for the experiment—a tiny pellet of deuterium."

"Wait a second," Rick burst in. "Containment field? Deuterium? Doesn't your dad use that to run the fusion reactors around here?"

"Yeah, with a whole lot of safeguards that won't allow the reaction I'm looking for."

"Maybe your dad knew what he was doing when he set those safeguards up." Rick appeared to be genuinely worried. "Let's face it, a fusion reactor is really a very tiny piece of the sun. I'd hate to see us get burned."

Tom stared at his best friend. "Do you really think I'd risk your lives like that?"

Rick and Mandy silently shook their heads.

"Trust me, guys. I'm using hardly any deuterium. My biggest problem was figuring out how to aim at such a tiny target. Besides, the computer simulations show that the energy from this zap will be focused *inward*. For a millionth of a second, on a very tiny scale, we'll duplicate the inside of a collapsing supernova."

Tom's eyes gleamed with suppressed excitement. "And then we'll have a teeny-tiny black hole."

"Great," Rick said. "And what will you do with it?"

Tom grinned again. "I'll find out what's on the other side." He pointed to another piece of equipment, a long robot arm with what seemed to be a very fine hair sticking out of one finger.

"That little whisker is an extremely thin optical fiber. You know how the phone companies use fiber optics to send information? Well, I've got the world's tiniest video camera mounted on the end of this fiber, just small enough to fit through my mini–black hole. With luck, we'll be able to get a look at whatever is on the other side."

"What are you expecting to see?" Mandy asked.

Tom shrugged. "Physicists have been arguing about what's on the other end of black holes since the theory was developed. They could lead into other parts of the universe, into other times, or even into other universes."

"Parallel worlds." Mandy nodded. "I've read about them a lot. They're universes just like ours, except somewhere in history, they branched off."

"So, if this gizmo works, we may get a snapshot of a dinosaur or a passing spaceship or how California would look if Napoleon had won at Waterloo," Rick said. "Or we may see nothing."

"I'm betting on nothing," Mandy suddenly said. "The ultimate Negative Zone."

"Why is that?" Rick asked.

"Remember, they call those things black holes," she said. "Their gravity is so strong, they even suck down light. I don't think that anything a black hole takes in will ever come out—and that includes the data flowing along that fiber-optic probe."

"We'll find out in a minute." Tom stepped from the equipment to his friends and hit a button. With a deep rumble, the remaining blast shields rolled in from the walls along their tracks, creating an unbroken barrier between the experiment vault and the control room where the three friends now stood. Tom rapped the shield. "The armor in these things is depleted uranium, the toughest stuff going. And the windows are Perspex-7. They can withstand a cannon blast."

"Why don't I feel better about this?" Rick muttered.

Tom pulled on a pair of coveralls and went to an equipment drawer.

"Better put these on," he said, pulling out three sets of heavily tinted goggles. "It will get a little bright in there." Then he motioned his friends to a set of chairs by the Perspex panels and headed for a control board.

"Let's get the target centered," he said, tapping a few keys. A robot arm swung down from the vault ceiling, holding a tiny pellet of fusion fuel in the center of the metal doughnut. Tom's fingers flicked over the control board, hitting switches. "Now for the containment field."

A bass-level hum kicked in. They could feel its vibration in their chests and stomachs. Tom flicked another switch. "I just connected the experimental apparatus to the fusion center's particle accelerator. Dad gave me the authorization for one zap . . ."

He pressed a button. "And it's coming now."

A new note rode over the hum, cycling higher and higher until it reached an earsplitting shriek. Then the lasers fired at each other, twin bolts of brilliant red flashing to hit dead-on in the center of the metal doughnut. The searing incandescence when the beams struck, even through the shielded goggles, was the best light show Rick or Mandy had ever seen.

Then the show went out of whack. Although the light beams kept flashing, they somehow disappeared about an inch from their original focus. They seemed to pour their energy into blackness. No, the blackness was an egg-size glowing globe.

Glowing? The light was hardly bright. It was dark, dark blue, almost a purplish black. It was an eye-tearing color they'd never seen before. Instinctively, they turned their eyes away from it, unable—or unwilling—to probe for whatever lay in the middle of the globe.

"I—I, uh, guess you did it," Rick said, letting his breath out. "How long will the hole last?"

"It'll close naturally when I cut out the

lasers," Tom said. He hit a switch, then frowned. "The lasers aren't cutting off." He slapped more switches, glancing at the gauges. "It's like that thing is sucking all the energy out of them."

"Tom!" Mandy said, staring through the Perspex panel. "The globe's getting bigger."

The blob of dark fire was now the size of a baseball, whirling inside the containment field. Its eerie glow was even harder to look at. So was the equipment. Its clean, straight lines seemed subtly curved, as if the universe had gone suddenly off-kilter. A trick of the light? Or had something gone seriously wrong with the universe within the blast doors?

Tom's face was tight as he keyed in a special code. A previously blank section of the control panel flipped up on hinges, revealing four red keys. The words EMERGENCY POWER DISCONNECT flashed in bright green letters on a small screen.

Tom slapped his hand down on all four switches. Nothing happened.

"The controls are shot," he said in a hoarse voice. "I'll have to do this manually."

"What are you talking about?" Mandy cried.

"I set up supersharp blades over the cables to the lasers. They would literally cut the power—if their motors worked. Now it looks like I'll have to chop them myself."

Tom leaped to an equipment closet and

swung a fire ax onto his shoulder. He pushed the controls that opened the blast doors. "Close these behind me," he ordered.

His words were whipped away in a sudden gale, as if the air in the control room were being sucked away. Tom realized that was exactly what was happening. The air in the vault was being pulled into a small, dangerously powerful black hole.

Tom headed for the far laser, moving as if he were fighting a whirlwind. He was. The wild breeze snatched at anything loose, sending it fluttering madly toward the black hole.

A rustling flight of papers flapped past Tom's ear, catching him by surprise. He glanced back and stumbled over a cable on the floor.

His shoulder hit the huge metal doughnut that projected from the containment field. It no longer contained anything. The bluish globe had moved out from the focus of the lasers.

Now it was almost a yard wide. And Tom Swift, off balance, was falling into it.

"Tom!" Mandy screamed as the blast doors clanged shut.

Tom couldn't answer her. The whole world around him had gone a ghastly blue. He thought he heard an explosion.

Then everything went black.

2

WHAT THE—" TOM SWIFT DIDN'T GET ANY FUR-
ther. He realized he couldn't hear the words
he was saying, anyway. They were all in his
head. There was no sound in the mad universe
swirling around him—only his soundless, terrified screams.

At first Tom thought the experiment vault
had disappeared, and he was hurtling through
empty space. All around him was that weird
nonlight, the light from the globe. That's
when he realized what must have happened.
The black hole! The thought crashed in his
head. I've gone through the black hole!

Tom stared around, eager to take in as
much as he could. He was in a strange new
world, someplace no human had ever been

before. It wasn't easy to make out objects—he felt as though he were moving at terrific speed. At first he could get only glimpses. But the more he saw, the clearer it became that everything around him was somehow wrong.

Tom had seen a lot of weird things—he couldn't miss them on the cutting edge of science. But never had his eyes taken in anything like he was seeing now. First, there was that dark fire—more painful to the eye than plain blackness. The sickly glow was like the phosphorescence on a piece of rotting wood. It was barely strong enough to show Tom just how twisted everything else around him was.

He seemed to be flung through space, tumbling through fields of stars. But these weren't the friendly twinkling dots of the night sky. They were dim, distorted shapes, barely less dark than the blackness beyond. As they wheeled past his view, they left faint, luminous trails—the way snails leave a track of slime.

Tom thought he passed a world. He wasn't sure. It looked like a modern art painting, with the artist deliberately distorting the perspective. Either that, or a giant had taken the planet in his hands and wrung it out.

Tom found the vision more than unsettling—the deformed world was downright terrifying. This was a sight humans were just not meant—or didn't have the eyes—to see. Tom went to bring his hand up over his eyes.

Far away—seemingly light-years beyond the planet—Tom caught a hint of movement. A twisted, tortured shape twitched. Then Tom realized he was seeing his own hand. The fingers were elongated, outlandishly thin and stretched, going off at impossible angles. Some of the bends came in places where there were no joints.

Scientist or not, Tom closed his eyes against the bizarre sight. *I guess Mandy had the right name for this place,* he thought as he tumbled on. *The Negative Zone. It's like no reality I've ever known.*

He shuddered, forcing himself not to think how his body must look, stretched, twisted, and bizarre. He really could go nuts if he let this place get to him. *Have to pull myself together,* Tom realized. *I've got to live through this and get back. But I can't do anything if I completely lose it.*

The mental pep talk worked. Tom calmed down and opened his eyes again.

Immediately, he wished he hadn't. Flashing past him in the perverted sky was a contorted parody of a human form. Some parts were enormously large, others ridiculously small. He had an awful suspicion some organs were inside-out. Was that a giant liver grossly pulsing out there?

Most disturbing was that the body floating by looked strangely familiar.

Tom didn't have time to keep staring as the horror flew off into the distance. He had something much more interesting to peer at. Far ahead of him, he could just make out a pinpoint of light—real light, not the unsettling antiglow that he'd been pinwheeling through.

The light at the end of the tunnel—that's how Tom immediately thought of the bright speck—was getting larger. Tom seemed to be rocketing toward it at incredible speed.

Maybe it *is* the light at the end of the tunnel, Tom thought. He remembered theories that black holes were actually tubes through the fabric of space and time—cosmic wormholes, one physicist had called them. In that case, what was at the other end?

He would find out in a moment.

Tom was spewed out into sudden, blinding brilliance. He felt a sickening wrench, smashed into something, and everything went black again.

An unknown amount of time later, Tom painfully pushed himself up on his hands and knees. His coverall was shredded, but otherwise he seemed all right. He was in bright sunlight, with the ruins of a wooden shack around him. The place had no roof, and it looked as if it had been hit by a tornado.

Tom glanced around, his head pounding. The shack appeared to have been used as some sort of lab. Among the wreckage he could see pieces of equipment. What is this stuff? he wondered. Then he saw the huge buss bars. Whatever experiment had been performed there had required high voltage. The heavy-duty conductors were used only for massive amounts of electricity, which would melt regular wires. Judging from the size of the metal slabs, Tom figured they must have been carrying enormous energy. Also scattered around the wrecked shack were gigantic hand-wired circuits, old-fashioned transistors, even some ancient vacuum tubes. This was the kind of equipment his dad would have used in an experiment.

Tom stepped through the doorway of the shack—the door itself had been blown out—and froze. He clung to the shattered doorpost, staring.

Tom knew the landscape, all right. He was in the California mountains, in a valley not too far from the town of Central Hills. Tom gazed at the surrounding hillsides, recognizing them all. He ought to—he lived there. Except that there was no trace of his house. And the valley that housed the huge Swift Enterprises complex was empty.

When he'd gone into the testing bunker, all the land for acres around was owned by his father's company, Swift Enterprises. On that land, Tom Swift, Sr., had developed the ultimate high-tech laboratory system. The many buildings forming the complex gave it the look of a small city, and hundreds of people worked there. Now Tom's shocked eyes took in a vista of sand and sun-dried grass, with the occasional cactus and yucca for variety.

Tom tottered away from the wreckage and plunked himself down on a boulder overlooking the valley. He didn't need binoculars to see that nothing lived down there, except maybe a few jackrabbits. The Swift complex was gone. Where was the fusion-power reactor, the labs, the manufacturing plants, the spaceport, the testing areas? Where was the bunker he'd been in?

Tom slowly eased his head down into his hands. Blood pounded in his ears, and his temples throbbed with pain. His head had been aching since he'd arrived here—wherever *here* was.

Could that explain things? Had he taken some sort of blow to the head that had scrambled his circuits? Maybe what he was seeing was a hallucination.

Tom rapped the boulder he was sitting on, then hurriedly blew on his knuckles. For a hallucination, the boulder felt painfully real.

That meant his gut-wrenching trip through the black hole had to have been real, but Tom's mind kept skittering away from the disturbing conclusion.

He'd been sucked into a black hole, and spit out right back home. No, Tom corrected himself. This place didn't look like *his* home, even if it was Central Hills.

He remembered Rick's half-serious joke about seeing dinosaurs or spaceships. Well, he hadn't gone that far in time. The wooden shack proved that there were people around.

Tom stared hard at the hills and bluffs, then at the floor of the valley. The land didn't seem much eroded, and since there was no trace of the huge, deep foundations of the fusion plant or the particle accelerator, he didn't think he'd landed in the future.

So, he'd been flung into the past. What could he expect? Cowboys? Conquistadors?

Tom shook his head, then grimaced in pain. His temples were still pounding. No, not with that scientific equipment around. He wasn't thinking straight, that much was certain.

What was he going to do? Whom could he turn to? This was a world where nobody even knew Tom Swift existed.

Tom's thoughts were interrupted by a loud clattering noise. "What now?" Tom said, rising from his rock. The noise wasn't doing his headache any good.

Then Tom stared as a helicopter rose into view from behind the far rank of hills. The aircraft was a museum piece, like something out of the 1950s. With a big Plexiglas dome in front and an openwork girder tail, it reminded Tom of a giant dragonfly.

The roar of the copter's engine and the *whik-whik-whik* of its revolving rotors was deafening.

Then an amplified voice boomed out. "We have you surrounded!" The words echoed off the stony hills.

Tom stood frozen, not believing what he was seeing—or the next thing he heard.

"Surrender, Thomas Swift. Surrender immediately!"

3

A UNIVERSE AWAY, ON THE OTHER SIDE OF A recently disappeared black hole, the air crackled in an underground bunker. The lights had died in a flash of ozone, and the equipment had exploded. There was no trace of movement in the experiment vault.

Rick Cantwell dashed through a thin opening between a pair of scarred blast shields. The heavily armored panels had been blown off their tracks. He felt lucky that the shields had been jarred apart. It would be some time before they opened automatically again.

He staggered into the experiment vault. The eerie blue glow from the experiment was gone. Now the huge vault was filled with smoke and the stink of burning insulation.

Smashed equipment lay crazily all over the room, tossed at random by the blast that had destroyed it.

"Is Tom all right? Do you see him?" Mandy stood by the opening in the shields, peering desperately toward the center of the room. "He had just fallen into that blue glow when everything went up." She brushed tears from her cheeks. "This all happened because he went in there to save us. He's got to be all right. He's *got* to."

Rick stared dubiously through the gloom. Tom was nowhere to be seen, but there was a big mound of wreckage on the spot where Tom had disappeared. It was as if the debris had been sucked to the site of the unearthly glow. "I'm afraid the glare of the blowing circuits cut through even those wonder goggles he gave us. I didn't see a thing."

Rick turned toward Mandy, his eyes stinging from the acrid smoke. "I, uh, think you should go get some help. It's a sure thing *I* can't move all this stuff."

Rick turned back to the bad-smelling haze still rising from the wrecked equipment, his face tight. What if the rescuers found a bloody mess instead of Tom Swift?

From behind him, he heard the ponderous groaning of the heavy steel bunker doors opening. "I'm on my way," Mandy shouted over her shoulder. "Keep looking, Rick. You've got to find him. Reinforcements are on the way!"

"Great!" Rick called after her. He pushed on into the devastated experiment vault. "Great," he said again, this time with a lot less enthusiasm. Wreckage had been flung all over the place, with very little open space for movement.

"I guess we didn't get a chance to see Tom's black hole—if he really created one. But he sure managed to create a supermess." Easing uncomfortably between mounds of debris, Rick halted as a fat blue spark leaped from one pile to another. "Oh, tremendous," he groaned. "Some of this stuff is still live."

As Rick made his way to the central mass of wrecked hardware, he halted. Not all the newly created junk was machinery. Rick could see a foot sticking out from the disaster area.

He stared hard in the half-light. Were his eyes playing tricks on him? Or was the foot actually stirring feebly?

"What's going on in here?" a loud voice boomed from the observation area. "Rick, why are you just standing there?"

Rick, still wary of live wires, turned to see a huge figure silhouetted between the open bunker doors. It bulked considerably larger than Rick's football player's build and stood a head and a half taller than his six foot height.

The figure was also definitely an *it*—sunlight from outside the bunker gleamed on the figure's metallic skin.

"Rob!" Rick yelled. This was exactly the help he needed. Tom had built his very own lab assistant, creating a robot with a human form. Rob was supposed to be the movement module of a portable computer system but had upgraded itself with numerous improvements. Saboteurs had gotten into the system during Tom's last adventure, turning Rob into a murder machine, and Tom had had to destroy his creation. Then he'd gone to work rebuilding Rob into his strong right arm.

Strong was the key word, Rick realized. With Rob's mechanical muscle, they stood a chance of freeing Tom from all this ruin before it crushed or electrocuted him.

The robot moved quickly along the narrow aisles among the destroyed equipment.

"Careful," Rick called. "The wires over there are still—"

"*Whooo!*" Rob exclaimed as an arcing discharge scorched his leg. "Still got some live circuits here, I see. Good thing Tom beefed up my insulation."

"We'll need all the help you can give," Rick told the robot. "Tom is trapped under this pile here. We've got to get him out."

"First, I'll clear us some space to work." Rob picked up a huge iron beam and tossed it aside.

Between them, they started working around the exposed foot. Rob knelt to stare into the wreckage. "I think he's lying in a small open pocket, with nothing pinning him down." The robot's photocell eyes gleamed brighter. "He's still breathing."

"But for how much longer?" Rick coughed as another cloud of smoke wafted past him.

He also realized that the throbbing hum of power hadn't cut off. "Rob," he asked, "is that noise supposed to keep going on when so much of the stuff here has been trashed?"

The robot paused in the middle of shoving aside a smashed metal partition. "Actually, no—it's dangerous," Rob stated. "We might have an explosion in here. Or a major discharge of the electric power."

"Discharge?" Rick said.

"Imagine an indoor lightning bolt." Rob's photocell eyes flashed. "I'm afraid that might be more than my insulation can handle—not to mention yours."

"Then let's hurry."

They went back to the job, tearing wreckage off the still form on the floor.

"Hey, in there." Another voice cut across the smoky gloom of the experiment vault. "Mandy said something went seriously wrong with this experiment. Is my son okay?"

Tom Swift, Sr., was already rushing through the gap in the blast doors. At first glance, his trim, lean form made him seem almost like a twin to his son. At second glance, though, the gray in his blond hair showed and so did the wrinkles around his eyes. Just then his face was deeply creased with worry.

"We think Tom's okay," Rick called. "But there's still a lot of loose electricity around here. Things may blow."

"We'll fix that," Mr. Swift said crisply. He glanced over his shoulder. "Krebbs, Walton— cut the main power lines to this bunker. And tell Harlan Ames to send in the damage-control team with heavy-duty equipment."

In moments, the ominous hum had disappeared, and emergency lights were being strung in the ruined vault. A rescue team in insulated suits arrived, led by the head of Swift security, Harlan Ames. The white-haired security chief wasn't there just to direct. He stepped right into the middle of the cleanup.

As Mandy arrived back at the bunker, she found her cousin Dan Coster and Tom's younger sister, Sandra, about to enter.

"I was at home, listening to Dan trying to play the guitar, when we heard that Tom totaled the lab." Sandra was trying to be casual, but her eyes were scared as she looked at Mandy. "He didn't really—did he?"

"What do you mean, 'trying to play'?" Dan tossed his head to get his long, curly hair out of his eyes. He, Mandy, and Sandra fell silent

23

as they stepped through the bunker's blast doors. "Hey, Tom-Tom!" Dan exclaimed when he saw the wreckage inside. "Wish my band could bring down the house like this!"

He glanced quickly at Sandra. "Sorry. Is Tom all right?"

"We're just about to find out," Rick called to them.

Dan, Sandra, and Mandy reached the work space as the last fused and blasted remnants of Tom's experimental apparatus were finally moved aside. Mandy gave a little scream when she saw the limp form revealed on the floor. Rick grabbed her arm as she staggered back.

"Oh, man," Dan said unsteadily. "This explosion must have been bad."

Tom lay pale-faced and unmoving, his clothing in rags.

"Get the stretcher in here!" Mr. Swift managed to keep his face calm, but his voice showed how concerned he was. "I want Tom in the hospital as soon as possible."

Mr. Swift didn't let anyone else take the job of moving his son. He picked up Tom and carried him in his own arms to the ambulance gurney waiting by the entrance.

The moment he was lifted from the ground, Tom junior stirred uneasily. His bloodshot eyes fluttered open, but they only stared unfocused at the ceiling. His arms made weak gestures, as if he were trying to ward off

24

something terrible. "Wrong, wrong—everything is wrong!"

Tom's voice was hardly more than a murmur, but his face showed deep horror.

"Tom! Are you all right?" Mr. Swift cradled his son protectively.

Rick and Mandy watched worriedly. Rob loomed behind them. Sandra clung to Dan's arm.

"Come on, Tom," Dan said, trying to lighten the mood. "Don't keep us in suspense."

Now Tom's eyes focused. He lay like a little child in his father's arms, staring up at Mandy. "W-who are you?" he breathed, gazing around at the wreckage uncomprehendingly. "Where am I?"

"Tom!" Mandy's voice was almost a sob. "Don't you remember what was going on? Don't you know who you are?"

The keen blue eyes that usually were so intent seemed confused now. "I'm Thomas Swift," he said weakly.

Worry etched another few years onto Tom senior's face. "Calm down, son. You're safe. You're with your father. We're taking you to the hospital."

Tom's face whipped back to his dad's as if his gaze had been pulled there by a string. "F-father?" he managed to gasp out.

Then he fainted dead away.

4

IN ANOTHER UNIVERSE, ANOTHER TOM SWIFT
stood gawking beside a ruined wooden shack.
He didn't gawk for long, though. One look at
the helicopter blaring threats was enough.

Tom whipped around and dashed away
from the direction the copter had come
from.

"He's running!" the angry voice behind him
boomed. "Move in, men!"

Tom started down the slope, then skidded
to a stop. The hillside below him was suddenly teeming with tiny figures dressed in
various uniforms—blue, khaki, and olive
drab.

Looks like a manhunt, Tom thought. I wonder who they're really after. From the way

26

they kept pointing and running in his direction, Tom got the feeling they were after *him.*

Then he heard bull-horned orders from below. "Come on, you dogfaces, close in on him. And get those guns out!"

Guns? Tom glanced toward the oncoming horde. One eager warrior raised a rifle to his shoulder. As the man took aim, Tom stumbled, his heel sinking into an eroded gully and sliding out from under him. The next thing Tom knew, he'd landed flat on the seat of his pants, just as a bullet whistled through the space where his head had been seconds before.

A ragged volley boomed out along the hillside as more members of the superposse added their firepower. A cactus off to Tom's right was shredded by wild shots.

Tom dove for the nearest cover he could find—a large clump of brush about ten feet downslope. Luckily, there were no thorns to greet him. But there was a surprise.

The brush in the center of the clump had been cut away. All that was left was a shell with a roof of greenery woven over it. Hidden beneath this screen was a car like none Tom had ever seen.

It was big, gray, and heavy-looking, with rounded lines that reminded Tom of cars he'd seen in old gangster movies. A long hood promised a huge mill of an engine, but the trunk of the car came to a point. The look of the car was definitely unusual, but it seemed to promise speed.

Speed was exactly what Tom needed just then—if he could get inside the car and start it. The door locks were no problem—the only key Tom needed was a straightened-out piece of wire from his pocket. The ignition lock didn't offer much challenge, either. Tom had no problem bypassing the lock and hot-wiring the car.

Under the long hood, the engine roared to very satisfying life. Tom put the car in gear and felt it lurch forward. "The machinery may be crude, but it's built for power," Tom said aloud.

The car tore through the screen of brush like a souped-up tank. Branches scattered, and so did a group of surprised police officers. Tom roared past the first line of law-enforcement types and jolted down the slope, aiming for a mountain road that snaked its way across the hillside.

There were still lots of people between Tom and the road. Tom recognized the uniforms of the local police, the California Highway Patrol, state troopers—and could those guys really be the National Guard?

Tom cringed behind the wheel as one guardsman shouldered a heavy carbine and emptied his magazine straight into the windshield.

Tom was giving himself up for dead, but the bullets bounced off as if they were hailstones. The car was armored!

More furious troopers came running. A crewcut agent in an FBI jacket triggered two shotgun blasts at the window. They merely rattled off, right by Tom's ear.

But as he reached the road, Tom saw one of the National Guard troopers lugging a heavy tube uphill. This guy was taking no chances—he was bringing a bazooka into the fight.

"Sorry, champ, I'm not hanging around to see if this car can handle *that*. And you guys don't look ready to listen to reason."

Tom floored the gas pedal, and soon he was flying down the road.

The troops were quickly left behind, but Tom was only too aware of the shadow that kept falling on the hillsides around him. The chopper was tailing him. As he drove deeper into the hills, though, the shadows kept growing longer.

"Good luck tailing me when the sun goes down," Tom told the circling helicopter.

It was almost as if the pilot had heard him. As the sun set, he tried a couple of fly-in-the face maneuvers, hoping to force Tom off the road. Tom tightened his grip on the steering wheel and kept on driving. Finally, as full dark set in, the chopper fell behind. Tom grinned as the helicopter's running lights disappeared behind a hill.

Okay, he told himself. There's a maze of roads through these hills. I can be miles from where they last spotted me. And if I'm careful and don't use my lights, I should be pretty hard to spot.

Tom jolted along rutted roads, gravel trails, and dirt tracks. He'd been heading for the desert when the chopper had given up the chase. Now he doubled back with a definite destination in mind: Central Hills. Once there, he could find out what was going on.

He turned onto a cracked and bumpy concrete strip leading into town. This should have been the main route to the Swift complex, a well-tended artery he'd often driven along. Instead, it was deserted and decaying. Clumps of vegetation grew from cracks in the pavement.

Almost at the town limits, Tom turned on his headlights. But instead of the sprawling housing developments he expected to find, Tom saw only sand flats and cactus.

The new business district was nowhere to be found, either. Where were the modest-size office towers? Tom found a few long, dilapidated buildings standing—or leaning—in their place. They looked like abandoned warehouses.

With no better destination, he drove on into

the town's original business district. Some of the mission-style buildings there had been around a long time. Tom had seen them in old photographs.

The ancient buildings were still there, but they hardly looked like the carefully painted tourist attractions Tom knew. The adobe brick hadn't been whitewashed for years. Many walls were spider-webbed with cracks. These buildings looked old, all right—old and forgotten.

Tom drove his car along quiet streets, searching for anything familiar. People sat on open porches, often fanning themselves. Hadn't they heard of air-conditioning? As he kept driving, Tom realized his car was getting a lot of stares. Compared to the handful of old clunkers parked in front of the houses, that wasn't surprising. But it made Tom feel conspicuous—not a good feeling for a fugitive.

At last, he pulled off the road and parked under a broken streetlight. The area seemed even shabbier than the rest of the town. Flimsy wood-frame buildings rose like three-story boxes. Beside some doors were faded signs: Morgan's Boarding House. Others were more straightforward: Rooms.

It was as good a neighborhood as any to abandon the car and disappear into the woodwork. Whoever this Thomas Swift the authorities were chasing might be, Tom knew he wasn't the guy. Maybe he'd just misheard the name. That loudspeaker had been blatting pretty loud. One thing was sure, though. Once he was away from this too-recognizable car, the cops wouldn't know him from Adam.

As he walked down the block, Tom let his mind go over the hints and clues he'd picked up since he'd been flung from the black hole: No Swift Enterprises, a sleepy village where Central Hills should have been, the crude technology of the helicopter, the car, and the wreckage he'd found in the shack.

Looks like I've been thrown into the past, Tom finally decided. Wish I could pin down exactly where I am.

"And now, the news," an amplified voice bellowed from a rickety open window. Tom headed closer. The wooden building seemed to be another flophouse. Somebody had left the radio blaring. Tom couldn't see into the room—the window was set just above his head.

The news announcer was going over the top story of the day. "Area residents are warned to watch out for archcriminal Thomas Swift, last seen driving a Cord Speedster east through the Redondo Hills. Swift has capped a notorious criminal career by working as a scientist-for-hire, building so-called suitcase atomic bombs for terrorist groups. Although federal agents managed to capture the bombs, the million-dollar payment, and the terrorists, Swift escaped. He is now number one on the FBI's Most Wanted list. Correspondent Don Fedlow interviews the agent in charge of the manhunt."

A new voice, a little higher-pitched than the anchorman's mellow bass, took over. "Special Agent Kennedy of the Antiterrorism Strike Force has recruited law-enforcement officers from all over Southern California to track down Thomas Swift. I understand additional ASF agents are flying in from Washington. Is that correct?"

Now a deep, grating voice came on. "That's right, Don. By dawn, we'll have an unbreakable dragnet surrounding the entire hills area."

"Do you have any advice for our listeners who may see Thomas Swift?" the newsman asked.

"Call the police. Do not, I repeat, *do not*, try to apprehend him yourself. He should be considered armed and dangerous. Very dangerous."

"Special Agent, you sound as if you've had some serious run-ins with Mr. Swift. Is that scar—"

"Swift gave it to me the last time I attempted to arrest him." A note of grim promise came into the voice. "This time we'll

33

get him and make sure he pays for all his crimes."

Tom cat-footed away from the window. A dragnet covering the entire area? A special task force out hunting? And the focus of this search was definitely Thomas Swift. Things didn't make sense. That name should have gone down in history—or infamy—if the guy had actually built A-bombs for terrorists. Why hadn't Tom ever heard of this evil Thomas Swift? Especially if he'd been hunted around Central Hills?

Tom pushed those thoughts aside. He had more pressing concerns. By dawn, the area would be crawling with cops, troops, and federal agents.

Maybe Tom—and that very recognizable car—should be farther away. He'd have a better chance of disappearing in a big city, anyway. This Central Hills was too small and isolated to make a good hiding place.

Tom turned to the car and froze. Maybe just parking the thing was a mistake. The car pulling up beside his gray speed-wagon looked like a bulbous antique, but the black-and-white paint job marked it clearly as a police cruiser.

Even as Tom watched, the driver's door opened, and a young police officer stepped into the street. The cop had a flashlight in his left hand. His right gripped the butt of his holstered pistol.

For a second, the reflected gleam of the flash illuminated the young cop's face.

Tom gawked. He knew that face almost as well as his own. It was Rick Cantwell!

He stumbled back in complete shock. As he did, his hip caught the side of an overloaded garbage can in the alley beside the flophouse. It overturned with enough clatter to raise the dead.

Above him, Tom heard a window shade rattle up. A figure stood in the window now, staring down at him.

Tom stared, too, into another familiar face. That was Mandy Coster leaning out the window!

Was he going out of his mind?

Maybe he was, because Mandy paid hardly any attention to him, calling out to Rick Cantwell instead.

"Hey, flatfoot!" she yelled. "Here's that Swift guy you've been looking for!"

In a mountain cabin, far away in the Colorado Rockies, a small, wiry man flipped off a radio. Sweat matted down his greasy hair. He pulled off his glasses and began fiddling with the wad of insulating tape wrapped around the nosepiece. "He's alive," he said in a thin voice. "The boss is still alive."

35

His partner, bigger and bulkier, shifted nervously on one of the bunks. "But, George—" His voice didn't match his body. It was high and piping, like a child's. "You said he was dead, that nobody could survive those weird lights and explosions."

The big man sounded almost disappointed and definitely frightened. His clear blue eyes clung to his partner's face. "He's not gonna be mad at us, is he?"

George, the skinny member of the team, had already rushed over to the rough-hewn dresser beside the bunks. He yanked the drawers open and began tossing clothes, both clean and dirty, onto the blanket.

"Go dig out our bags, Len," he told his friend. "I thought we'd be safe in this joint, but now we have to pack and get out of here—right away."

Len, big and slow, blinked his eyes in surprise. "But I thought we were going to stay here until the heat died down, George. You wouldn't even go out to get your glasses fixed. Where will we—"

"We're going to find the boss, Len." George's eyes, magnified by the thick lenses of his glasses, showed pure fear. "It might go better for us if we look for him—before he comes looking for us."

5

RICK CANTWELL TURNED FROM THE CAR TO Tom Swift. "All right, you. Freeze!"

Rick's voice held no trace of recognition, much less friendship, as he glared at Tom. Instead of a best friend's smile, all Tom saw was a professional law officer's face—grim and tight under the blue uniform cap.

Tom also noticed that as Rick charged across the street, he'd pulled the gun from his holster. It looked like a small cannon.

No time to talk this through, Tom thought. I'm out of here.

He leaped for the windowsill just above him and pulled himself into the room. Mandy Coster jumped back with a gasp as Tom scrambled into her dingy little room.

Tom stood facing Mandy—it *was* Mandy, unless she had a twin sister she never talked about. No, those big brown eyes, that chestnut hair, this was no look-alike. Tom had hung around with her long enough to be sure.

Or was he? This girl was staring at him as if she'd never seen him before. The big brown eyes were slitted in suspicion, the full lips a thin line.

Tom looked at her more closely. All the details were wrong. The girl in front of him had a teased mane of hair. Mandy never wore hers like that. Nor did she slather on so much lipstick. And her body seemed skinnier, tighter, pinched.

Then there were her clothes! Mandy might be described as a California girl, but she had never gone in for the beach bunny look. This Mandy wore a pair of tiny, tight white shorts and a skimpy T-shirt that left most of her deeply tanned midriff bare. Tom stared. Was that a tattoo above her navel?

The suspicious look on Mandy's face disappeared. Now she was goggling at Tom.

"Holy crow!" she screeched. "I only yelled that stuff to get a rise out of that cop. But it's really true! You *are* Thomas Swift!"

She was literally jumping up and down as she shouted. Maybe she didn't know Tom, but the thought that he was Thomas Swift certainly seemed to impress her.

"Thanks for all that yelling," Tom told her. "Now you've got the law after me."

Even as he spoke, they heard scrabbling at the window. Rick Cantwell had ditched his flashlight to get a hand free to climb over the sill. His other hand clutched his huge police-issue pistol.

As soon as Rick appeared in the window and started swarming in, Mandy snatched something from the top of a dresser. She dashed toward Rick, swung, and Tom heard a dull thud. Rick had time for only a quick groan before he was falling back out the window to crash into the garbage cans on the pavement.

"What was that?" Tom asked.

"My little equalizer." Mandy turned from the window to display a nine-inch-long black-jack. "Don't travel anywhere without it."

Tom was now convinced that this was not the girl he knew. He'd never seen Mandy in a bikini, so he couldn't be sure about the tattoo, but Mandy would *never* carry a blackjack.

"Who are you?" Tom asked.

"Mandy Coster," the girl replied.

"Mandy? Then what are you doing here?" Tom couldn't help it. The words just tumbled out of his mouth.

Mandy gave him a perplexed look. "I live here. What did you think—"

She was interrupted as the flimsy door to the room flew open.

"What's going on in here? Why all the noise? And who's this joker?"

Tom grabbed the top of the dresser to stay on his feet. He'd just had too many shocks in the last few minutes.

Now he was getting another one. He knew the guy bursting through the door—it was Dan Coster, Mandy's cousin. Or rather, it was Dan's sleazy twin. The Dan Tom knew would never be taken for a white-bread kind of guy. He played in a rock band, partied a lot, and his curly black hair was on the long, wild, and free side.

This Dan was even wilder. His greasy hair was pulled back in a ponytail—much longer than Tom had seen the day before—and he had a big, black mustache. The thing that made the biggest impression on Tom, though, was the switchblade knife in this Dan's hand.

Dan stood in the doorway, staring. "Wait a minute. You're that Swift guy. Every cop in the world is chasing you." He rolled his eyes. "Oh, I don't believe it. This is why you're screaming, Mandy?"

Mandy shrugged. "Actually, I was screaming because of the cop I just slugged."

Tom watched as Dan's mustache actually

bristled. "Slugged? Did I hear you right? You *slugged* a cop?" Dan was very upset as he stared out the window. At least he snapped the knife blade back into its handle.

He glanced at Tom. "So what did you do? Off him?"

"Off?" Then Tom realized what Dan meant. "No, I didn't kill him. Why—"

But Dan was already shrugging it off. "Hey, *I'm* glad. It's just not the way you usually act, as far as I've heard."

He stepped away from the window. "In fact, I don't believe you guys," Dan went on. "First you"—he whirled on Tom—"climbing in my cousin's window. Then you"—now he glowered at Mandy—"rattling that cop's brains. It's not enough that the cops in this burg are on our backs all the time. You want them to—"

"I have a suggestion," Mandy said. "Let's get out of town."

"No way." Dan shook his head decisively. "I've got a hog in pieces all over the floor of the garage in back."

"A hog?" Tom said in disbelief.

"He means a motorcycle," Mandy translated. "Dan, we can't hang around here discussing things. That cop is going to be back on his feet in a couple of seconds."

"So, how are we supposed to get out of here?" Dan demanded.

"I've got a car," Tom suggested. "Right now, I want to get back to it as soon as possible. I don't know if Rick radioed in about the car before he checked it out."

"You know Uptight Cantwell?" Dan said. "Hey, Swift, you get around."

"Right now, I think we should be getting out of here." Mandy went to the dresser and stuffed a few things into a shoulder bag. "Anything you want to bring?"

Dan shrugged. "I'm wearing it."

"Then let's blow this candy stand." Dan turned to the door, but Mandy dashed to the window. She threw a leg over the sill, then the other. After teetering for a moment, she slithered down to the pavement below.

Tom ran to the window and saw Rick Cantwell rising to his knees. That was before Mandy got to him and decked him again. She grinned and slipped the blackjack into her shoulder bag.

"Well, what are you waiting for?" Dan Coster said. "Follow the babe."

Tom jumped from the window, with Dan right on his heels. They ran to the long gray car and piled in. The empty police cruiser was still double-parked beside it.

The three kids all crammed into the front seat. Dan stared with interest as Tom hotwired the engine into life. "Why didn't you use your key?"

"Couldn't find it," Tom admitted.

"Well, you did a pretty nice job," Dan said. From his tone of voice, Tom figured he took a professional interest in this sort of thing.

There wasn't time to discuss the finer points of hot-wiring, though. In the distance they could hear the wail of sirens.

"I think they're coming our way," Mandy said a little nervously.

"Then we'll head the other way." Tom popped the clutch, hit the gas, and tore down the empty sidestreet.

In moments, they were out of town, bombing along dusty country roads.

"Where to?" Dan asked.

"Los Angeles," Tom replied. "And the fastest way to get there and put some distance between us and the cops is the freeway."

The big city would offer lots of places for Tom to hide. With luck, a freeway getaway would also put Tom well beyond the reach of the police dragnet. Let the searchers concentrate around the hills. Tom Swift wouldn't be there for them to find.

Unfortunately, the sound of the sirens didn't grow fainter behind them. They came on, even as Tom whipped down the entry ramp to the freeway.

"They want a chase?" Tom said through gritted teeth. "I'll give them a chase."

Tromping hard, he pushed the gas pedal to the floor.

The powerful engine snarled under the long gray hood. Tom, Dan, and Mandy were all pushed back in their seats as the car streaked forward like a beast unleashed.

If anything, however, the sound of sirens grew louder.

"Sounds like the boys in blue have called in reinforcements," Mandy said. She twisted to look back through the rear windshield. "Uh-oh, here they come. Lots of blinking cherry lights."

"Oh, great." Tom glanced back, too.

"Hey! Watch it!" Dan yelled.

Tom braked, but he was too late to stop the car. It tore through a set of wooden trestle barriers.

"What's going on here?" Tom said. "Some kind of roadblock?"

"What for?" Dan looked right, then left. "Why would they set up an unmanned road-block? Especially all these miles out of town. I've never been this far along the freeway."

Then Tom saw why Dan had never come that far and why there wasn't any other traffic on the road.

This freeway wasn't exactly the twin to the one that Tom used back home in Central Hills. Apparently, in this world the state of

California hadn't come along as fast in building its highway system.

It certainly hadn't built the bridge that Tom expected to be speeding across.

The pavement led right to the lip of a deep arroyo and started again thirty feet away.

In between, though, was thirty feet of empty space.

DAN COSTER BRACED HIS ARMS AGAINST THE dashboard, yelling, "Holy—"

The rest of his shout was drowned out by the screech of brakes. The long gray car swerved, but Tom managed to keep control and stop it three feet short of where the freeway ended.

"W-what do we do now?" Mandy finally managed to say. "No road ahead of us, and a million cops coming up behind. We've had it."

"Maybe not." Tom threw the car into reverse, backed up, then turned the car round. They were roaring along the freeway, heading back the way they'd come.

They could see dozens of headlights coming

46

toward them, with lots of red flashers and screaming sirens.

"If you think playing chicken with the cops is going to do anything—" Mandy began.

"Hang on," Tom interrupted.

He sent the car squealing into a U-turn, then floored the accelerator. The long gray car fishtailed a little, then took off like a rocket, bumping along the rough concrete roadway. Ahead, the unbridged gap came rushing toward them.

"Oh, no," Mandy said as she realized what Tom was trying to do. *"No!"*

She and Dan braced themselves against the dashboard again. Tom held tight to the steering wheel, his eyes on the speedometer. They'd have to be pushing 100 for this to work. The needle crept up. He saw a knob marked SPCH and yanked it out. The engine's low, throaty growl changed to a high-pitched whine, almost like a jet engine's. The needle hit 100.

The engine was howling under the hood now as the car streaked along the last few yards of roadway. Mandy's yell burst out in wild harmony as they left the ground and hurtled through thin air.

They were across the gap and jolting down on the other side almost before they knew it. Mandy was quiet now, her face pale, her knuckles white where they clutched at the dashboard.

Dan Coster let out a loud whoop and pounded on his section of the dash. "Way to go, Swift. I've got to hand it to you. It must be great to know exactly what your car can do."

"I—I wasn't sure." Tom managed to relax his grip on the wheel. They were now zooming along the section of new freeway. Tom slowed the car. No use plunging at full speed into whatever other construction surprises lay ahead. "At least we've lost the cops for a while."

Behind them, at the lip of the nonexistent bridge, they could hear the mass scream of brakes.

Dan chuckled as he glanced back. "You sure ditched them, Swift." He stared at Tom, a little surprised. "Funny, I never pegged you for the modest type—not from what I've heard, anyway. So how come you said you didn't know if this road rocket would make it across that gap?"

"I really *didn't* know," Tom admitted.

"Come on, man," Dan said in disbelief. "Everybody knows about Thomas Swift and his supercharged Cord."

Tom glanced over at Dan. Cord? Nobody had manufactured that make of car for decades. When was he? He couldn't be in the past, not when he kept bumping into people he knew—even if they didn't know him.

"Dan," Tom said as they drove along. "Do me a favor."

"Hey, anything," Dan said with a broad grin.

"What's today's date?"

Dan shrugged. "It's after midnight, so it's June fifth. I guess you lost track with all that running around, huh?"

June fifth. Tom had started his experiment on June fourth. "What year is it?"

Dan gave him a sidelong glance. "You sure you're okay, Swift? I mean, most people manage to remember what year it is."

Tom met the worried eyes. "Humor me, Dan."

Dan told him the year. Tom nearly swerved off the road. It was the same year he'd left.

"Okay," he muttered to himself as he got the car back on track. "I didn't travel back in time—I went sideways. This must be a parallel universe, just like the one I came from—except for a few things."

He kept his eyes on the road, thinking. Looks like technology here has lagged behind the world I know. My friends are a lot weirder, and I seem to be the most feared criminal in the world.

"Sideways?" Mandy spoke up. "Parallel universes?"

"Guys," Tom said, "I have a confession to make. I'm not Thomas Swift."

49

"Yeah, right." Dan began laughing. "You just happen to look exactly like him and drive around in his car."

"My name is *Tom* Swift. I live in Central Hills, near the Swift Enterprises complex, with my family."

"Swift hasn't got any family," Dan Coster objected. "And he sure doesn't live in a hick burg like Central Hills."

Mandy had been very quiet, staring at Tom and listening intently. Now she asked, "Where is this Swift Enterprises complex?"

"In the big valley up in the hills," Tom told her.

"You mean White Sand Valley?" Dan scoffed. "Nothing there but prairie dogs."

"Knock it off, Dan," Mandy said. "Maybe it's different where this Tom comes from."

Tom turned to her, a little surprised.

Mandy gave him an embarrassed smile and dug something from her shoulder bag. She held up a digest-size magazine with the title *Astonishing Stories*. It had a brightly colored cover featuring an astronaut in the clutches of an alien. The creature combined the worst features of a scorpion, an octopus, and a rutabaga. Yellow letters beside the picture read: "Special novel this month—The Universe Next Door!"

"I read a lot of science fiction," Mandy admitted. "They're always talking about alternate universes." She shrugged. "The Thomas Swift I read about in the papers is supposed to be some kind of science whiz—maybe smart enough to get between those universes."

She looked long at Dan. "But the guy we've met is nothing like the Thomas Swift we've heard about. This Swift is no killer, and I just don't think he's Thomas Swift."

Dan was shaking his head. "So, *Tom*, you come from one of these whozewhatsits—alternate universes. And you live here in Central Hills."

"I spent the last five years growing up with you," Tom said. He tapped Dan on the arm. "You had the mumps in fourth grade."

Dan stared. "How did you know that?"

Tom laughed. "Because you gave them to *me*." Then he looked at Mandy. "You came here on a visit when you were nine years old."

"That's right," Mandy said, amazed.

"In my world, your cousin and I didn't treat you too well. We taught you to make water balloons, then used all of them on you, until you were soaked."

Mandy giggled. "I could see Dan doing that."

"No way," Dan said. "My old man would have whipped my—" He cut off the words, looking a little sad. "He was a great guy before the accident."

"Accident?" Tom asked.

"Dan's dad died in a fire at the furniture factory when Dan was only twelve years old," Mandy explained.

Tom was silent. In his world, Dan's father was still alive.

Dan nodded sadly. "Things got real tight after that. Last year, when Mom got sick . . ." His voice got bitter. "We didn't have the bucks to pay the doctors."

Tom's hands tightened on the wheel. He remembered the delicate surgery Mrs. Coster had undergone in the past year. Swift Enterprises doctors and an innovative new treatment had saved her life. But it hadn't happened here.

"I quit school, trying to earn some money to help Mom. Worked as a mechanic in a service station. Didn't make enough, though. Since then, I've been bumming around," Dan said.

"And I blew into town a couple of months ago," Mandy spoke up. "After I ran away from home."

Tom gawked. "You're a runaway?" In his universe, Mandy had recently moved to Central Hills with her family.

"My dad's business went belly-up," Mandy said. "I overheard my folks talking about what to do with me. Money was really short, and they thought I'd be better off away from home."

She grimaced. "That meant a state orphanage. I decided if I had to leave, I'd do it my own way." She shrugged. "So I took off."

As they'd been talking, Tom had been working to put lots of distance between them and the cops they'd left behind. At the first chance, he'd exited from the freeway. On it, they would be too easy to track. Besides, there might be other nonexistent bridges.

On the local roads, he'd moved east as well as south. His original route had been like a big arrow pointing to L.A. Now Tom wanted to veer away from where the searchers would congregate.

As the eastern horizon began to lighten, Tom saw the tall sign of a motel silhouetted against the dawn.

" 'Cabins available,' " he read. "This is what we want."

Pulling up out of sight of the motel office, he turned to Dan. "You'll have to register for us. I don't want anyone to know that I'm around. If I can, I want to keep the car out of sight."

"Gotcha." Dan got out of the car, then hesitated. "They'll probably want to see the color of my money, and I haven't got much."

Tom reached into his pocket, then stopped.

"Great. I don't have much, either. And what I've got might look counterfeit."

"Wait a minute." Mandy popped up on her knees, bending over the back of the seat. "I saw a couple of suitcases back here."

She went to work opening one case tucked beneath the front seat. Tom went to work on the other.

Mandy shook her head. "I don't know what this stuff is. Maybe a radio set?"

Tom glanced over at the box full of electronic gear. "We'll check that later." He popped the locks on the second case. "We've got clothes and—whoa!"

Searching between layers of shirts, he turned up a thick bundle of paper money. "Fifties and twenties," Tom said, handing over a sheaf of bills to Dan. "We have lots of worries, but money won't be one of them."

Slipping the wad into his pocket, Dan headed for the office. He came back a few minutes later, waving a set of keys. "We've got the last cabin out, nice and far from the road."

They drove over to the isolated cabin, and Dan opened the door. "Well, come on. Let's move our luggage in."

Mandy took the bag with the clothes and money. Tom lagged behind with the suitcase full of electronic gear. "Stupid thing must weigh a ton," he muttered as he came through the door.

The cabin was small and snug—two bedrooms with a living room in between. Tom set the case down on a table and opened it again.

"I don't believe this!" he exclaimed, pulling out a bulky keyboard and tiny monitor. "This is a homemade portable computer!"

"Computer?" Mandy said. "They're big, house-size things." She rapped her magazine. "Except in sci-fi stories."

"A portable computer?" Dan scoffed.

Tom hefted the case. "Would you call sixty pounds portable?" He closed it up, yawning. "I'll look at this tomorrow. Now I want to hit the sack."

"Noooooooo!" Tom Swift's voice was a hoarse yell as he swam back to consciousness. His body, covered in cold sweat, was tangled in the bedclothes.

Dan Coster sat up in the other bed, staring at Tom with bleary eyes. "You know, Swift, this is the third day we've been here. And every morning, you wake me up the same way. What's the problem? Bad dream?"

Tom frowned, shaking his head. "I—I don't remember. But I can't shake this feeling that I'd better get home soon." He sighed. "If I only knew how. I think I'll spend the morning taking another crack at that portable computer."

He'd spent the last two days trying to unlock the codes to make the computer work. Tom had also worked with Dan, changing the color of the Cord.

"Okay. While you hit the keyboard, I'll get some supplies in town," Dan said.

Tom spent a frustrating morning. "Sixty pounds of aggravation," he muttered hours later. Tom banged his fist on the table. The vibration must have shaken something loose inside the computer, because words suddenly flickered onto the screen.

"When I step through the portal, it's probably a one-way trip," Tom read. "The universe doesn't like having paths torn through it. Whatever connection I make will probably heal over within a week. After that, even if I can rebuild my apparatus, I'll return to another universe, not the one I left from. As the guy says, 'You can't go home again.'"

The words faded from the screen, leaving Tom staring in shock. His evil alter ego had a point. How long would the hole he'd punched between universes keep them connected? A week? Less? He could be trapped here forever. . . .

"Still stuck?" Dan asked, coming through the door. "I could use a hand out there."

"Yeah, sure. Right now, I don't think I can face any more of this computer."

Dan had been the one to suggest repainting

the car. After Tom finished masking the chrome, he watched Dan go to work spraying. Two seconds of looking told Tom that Dan was quite practiced at car painting. "You've done this before, haven't you?"

Dan's face was hidden under a filter mask, but his eyes twinkled. "Let's just say most of the other cars I've painted were a lot hotter."

By evening, the car was done, and Tom at last began breaking through the system defenses Thomas Swift had planted in his homemade computer.

"Cracking the code, huh, Tom?" Mandy asked.

He shook his head. "I should have psyched out this strategy long ago." Still, Tom was grinning as the system came up on his alter ego's computer.

"Hey, Swift." Dan stepped into the living room, where Tom was hunched over the keyboard. Dan pulled a folded magazine from his back pocket and tossed it to Tom. It unfolded in midair and fluttered to the table. Tom saw the familiar cover of a weekly news magazine, with his face scowling from it. "Villain of the Year," the headline read. Across the bottom of the page were the words, "Million-dollar reward for Thomas Swift."

"Better watch it, Tom," Dan said. "The feds are offering a cool million to anyone who turns you in."

Tom laughed as he thumbed through the issue. Apparently, the manhunt for Thomas Swift was big news. "What do you know?" Tom said. "Thomas Swift had a couple of henchmen who seem to have disappeared." He stared at the picture of the two—Len Dinwiddie, hulking, not too bright. The caption under his picture was "The Muscle." The other guy, George Finn, was skinny, with a pinched face and dark, greasy hair—a nerd gone wrong. His caption was "The Technician." Tom kept flipping, then stopped when he reached the background story. " 'Thomas Swift: Profile of a Sociopath,' " he read aloud.

"What's a sociopath?" Dan asked.

"It's a guy who never understands that society's rules apply to him—a criminal with absolutely no conscience." Tom kept reading even as he spoke. "Whoa. I begin to understand a lot more about this world."

"Why?"

"It says here that Thomas Swift's parents both died when he was a little kid. An explosion on a test rocket." Tom shook his head. How would he feel if his folks had died like that? he wondered. The article said Thomas was an only child, so the disaster had happened even before his sister, Sandra, was born.

He read on. "Oh, wow. The shock of the accidents did in Thomas's grandfather. There was nobody left to run Swift Enterprises. The lawyers took over, and the company went down the tubes."

Dan dropped onto the sofa. "What happened to Thomas Swift?"

"He wound up penniless, a ward of the state. Then, as he got older, he turned to a life of crime to get back at the people he thought had cheated him. He came up with a bunch of phony inventions to con money out of rich people."

Tom grinned. "Then one—a lightweight laser—worked. Thomas used it to cut into bank vaults." He read on through a list of high-tech scams, robberies, kidnappings, even a murder.

"They say here, 'Swift is the most brilliant, twisted, and dangerous criminal of the century—maybe of all time.' " Tom frowned. "No wonder he didn't mind building a set of suitcase nukes for those terrorists. I'm just glad they caught those guys and the bombs."

"Well," Dan said, "they didn't catch Swift. Where do you think he got to, Tom?"

Tom's frown deepened. He'd thought a lot about that lately. There had been no trace of anyone around the smashed-up shack in the hills, but Thomas Swift's trademark Cord had been hidden nearby. If he'd tried to escape on foot, he should have been picked up by the converging law officers.

So where did Thomas Swift go?

Tom's mind went back to his nightmare journey through the Negative Zone. Along the way, he'd passed a horrifically twisted, yet strangely familiar shape. What if the black hole that had plunged Tom here had somehow picked up Thomas Swift? Suppose his evil twin was now in Tom's home universe? Tom now knew what horror Thomas Swift had caused here. His stomach tightened as he thought of what Thomas Swift could be up to back home. Then Tom remembered the message he'd read on Thomas's primitive computer: "Whatever connection I make will probably heal over within a week." Beads of cold sweat blossomed on the back of his neck. What if Thomas had been right?

"I don't know where Thomas Swift is." A V-shaped crease appeared between Tom's eyebrows.

"And I'm scared."

7

I'M SCARED," MANDY COSTER SAID TO RICK Cantwell. She slumped in the passenger seat of Rick's classic red Jaguar XKE as they drove through the gates of Swift Enterprises.

"Running a little rough," Rick said in embarrassment to the gate guard as the Jaguar let off a thunderous backfire.

"It *always* runs a little rough," the guard replied as he waved them through.

"Seriously, Rick," Mandy said, "I'm worried about Tom. He seems like a different person since that accident in the bunker. Even an easygoing guy like my cousin Dan is asking what the story is."

"Well, he hit his head or something in the explosion." Rick tried to sound calm, but his face showed concern. "There doesn't seem to be any physical damage the doctors could find. But I guess amnesia is no joke, even if they say it's only temporary."

Mandy bit her lip. "Don't you think it's odd that Tom doesn't know anybody at all?"

Rick could only shrug. "This amnesia stuff is pretty strange."

"It seems fake to me," Mandy said. "There's a funny look in Tom's eye."

"He's always got a funny look in his eye when he looks at you," Rick tried to joke.

Mandy didn't laugh. "You know, the first time we were alone, he came on really strong. I almost had to fight him off." The color rose in Mandy's cheeks. "I mean, Tom's never acted like that before."

Rick shrugged again as he pulled the car into a parking spot by the administration building. "I know what you mean. When he heard we were best friends, he carried on like my long-lost brother. It's as if Tom never had friends before and didn't know how to act."

They were both shaking their heads as they walked through the building entrance. Rick led the way across the lobby to a private elevator. He pulled a data-key from his pocket and slipped it into a slot. The doors parted, and Rick led Mandy into the cab.

"Well, we haven't seen him at all for the

last few days. Ever since he got out of the hospital, he's just about locked himself in his lab." Rick gave a little grin. "After he asked Rob and Orb how to get in."

The elevator let them out into a small room facing a huge metal door that would have looked more at home on a bank vault. Mandy reached out instinctively to place her hand in the outline of a handprint set in the center of the door.

Rick grabbed her wrist. "Yeesh! Do you want to set off every alarm in the place? That palm-lock opens the door only if Tom, his dad, or I press our hands there."

Rick put his hand against the outline, which glowed green and unlocked the door. Then he led Mandy down a corridor until they faced another metal door, this one with a speaker in its center.

"Name an Irish rock group named after an American spy plane," a mechanical voice boomed out.

"Music trivia?" Mandy said in disbelief.

The door speaker asked the question again.

Mandy gave Rick a look and whispered, "U2."

"Me, too?" Rick repeated. The door swung open.

"It's just a test for my voice pattern," he said as she sauntered in.

The room that was revealed to their view

was big enough to hold a full-court basketball game. Lab tables were placed around the room, but most of the usual clutter—unfinished inventions, repair jobs, test equipment—had been banished to the walls and corners. Even the calculations wall, with its equations and irreverent graffiti, was scrubbed clean.

Rick glanced at Mandy, feeling a chill. It was as though another personality had taken over the lab, clearing away the paraphernalia as parents clear away a kid's toys.

Tom Swift had his back to the door. He was hunched over a lab table, an untidy pile of science texts spread out in front of him. Beside him stood Rob, whose metal body gleamed. Across the table was a silvery globe about the size of a basketball. That was Orb, the computer-interface part of Tom's robotic invention, also recently repaired.

Orb bounced on the table as Tom slammed a book in frustration. "I keep reading and reading." He smashed another pile of science books over. "It's like trying to absorb twenty years of research in a week."

"Perhaps you should try a more systematic approach," Orb's quiet, reasonable voice suggested. "Outline your knowledge, then perhaps I can match some appropriate texts—"

"You don't understand what this world is like!" Tom exclaimed. "So far ahead—"

Rob turned toward the doorway. "Hi, Rick, Mandy."

Whipping around in his seat, Tom faced them with a tight face and suspicious eyes. His mouth was a bloodless line, grim and nasty. "What are you doing here?" he demanded. "How did you get in?"

"Well, uh—" Rick floundered. "I'm one of the people with access to the lab. The security system has me in it." He stopped uncomfortably. "I guess you don't remember."

"Hey, man, I didn't mean to jump down your throat like that." Tom gave Rick a big, beaming smile.

Mandy wondered if Tom had been practicing that smile in a mirror. It just didn't look real. The Tom she knew and liked was more quiet, laid-back, not always acting.

Tom threw an arm around Rick's shoulders, then did the same to Mandy. "I know you guys are probably a little worried about me shutting myself up in here." He squeezed a little tighter. Mandy squirmed in discomfort.

"It's just that I'm still working at getting myself together, checking things out, trying to piece together that last experiment. Seeing what I can remember—"

He cut himself off with a huge sigh. "I need

some time to myself. This knock on the head has been tough going."

Releasing his friends, Tom swayed a little bit, raising a hand to his forehead. "Wow, my head's hurting now. Too much excitement, seeing you guys."

Rick and Mandy shared puzzled glances. If Tom wasn't feeling well, why was he reading all those books and getting upset? Why wasn't he resting?

Tom looked over to Rob and gestured with his head. The robot came over, stepping between Tom and his friends. Tom made his way back to his chair with a dramatically unsteady gait.

"Tom seems a little tired now," Rob said as Tom sank into the chair. "Maybe you should cut him a little slack. What he needs is some rest, don't you think?"

"I guess so," Mandy said.

She and Rick really didn't have much of a choice. Rob was gently shooing them back out the door.

"You take it easy, okay, Tom?" Rick called from the door.

"Feel better," Mandy added. She felt a little foolish and angry, too. Was she mistaken, or had Tom just brushed them off?

"Thanks, guys." Tom managed a languid wave from the chair and gave them another of those bright, phony smiles. "Just let me get it together. I'll catch up with you guys soon, real soon. I promise."

He kept smiling and waving until the door closed. Then he dropped his hand and the friendly expression from his face.

"Orb," he snapped, "who else can get through those doors?"

"Only Rick, Tom. And, of course, your father. Mr. Swift has access to all doors." Orb had to raise his mild voice to be heard over the sound of Tom's impatiently drumming fingers.

"Well, I want you to fix it so nobody has access here except me. Cancel everybody else. I don't want anybody coming in—and bringing their ditzy friends."

A quiet chime rang out from a corner of the room. Tom whipped around. "What's that?"

"The laser printer has finished running off that job you wanted," Rob said.

"The printout on all the projects Swift Enterprises is working on?" Tom said. "Bring it here."

The robot headed over to the laser printer and came back with a sheaf of paper several inches thick.

Tom stared at all the pages. "The company does all that? I should have asked for a brief summary."

A mild crackle of static came from Rob's speakers, as if he were clearing his throat. "Tom, this *is* the brief summary."

Sighing, Thomas Swift began to riffle through the thick report. "Manufacturing operations. Shipbuilding and submersible operations. You guys make submarines. Aeronautics. *Space* operations? You've got to be kidding me!"

He ran a finger to the budget and bottom-line figures for that division, and his eyes went wide. "You put that kind of money in and get that kind of return? Outrageous!"

Whipping through more pages, he was less impressed. "Ecological operations—saving rain forests, endangered species. Who cares? Educational technology. Criminal rehabilitation—" He laughed out loud. "Oh, if those poor straights only knew!"

He stopped short when he came to another division, farther down in the pile. "Military equipment and armaments—not much money goes in here. But look at the projects—orbital lasers, particle weapons, invisibility suits, personal armor. What's this? Matter transmission?"

Letting the pages fall together, Thomas Swift straightened the pile, then leaned back in his chair.

He stared up at the ceiling, his eyes a little

unfocused. "This company is pretty amazing." Thomas Swift's voice was quiet, thoughtful.

"With all the hardware here behind him, a guy could end up ruling the world."

8

TOM SWIFT SAT AT THE SMALL DINING-ROOM table of the motel cabin. His eyes burned as he stared hard at the diagram on the computer screen.

He'd spent hours digging the secrets of Thomas Swift from the portable computer, feverishly racing against time to find out how to duplicate his evil alter ego's last experiment. He now knew how Thomas Swift had built the terrorists' bombs. He'd been in on the job from the beginning, helping them plan an attack on a breeder reactor.

From the notes, Tom realized that Thomas Swift had taken more than money for the job. His evil twin had also been paid in nuclear material. When the feds swooped down,

Thomas Swift had left the cash but taken the nuclear fuel slugs with him.

Now that Tom was in the file for Thomas Swift's last experiment, he understood why. According to the notes, Thomas Swift had been working on something he called the space warp.

Thomas Swift's notes were clear. "After this last caper, I'll probably be the most hated man in America. The borders will be closed, and I'll be hunted down like a dog. My only chance is to go somewhere else."

Although he wasn't sure where his "cosmic portal" would lead, Thomas Swift had gathered equipment in California for an ultimate escape.

"Found the perfect hideout—a real rube town," Swift had written. "Work going well."

Now Tom was going over the circuit diagrams for the equipment that Thomas Swift had built.

"Dangerous," Tom muttered as he envisioned the machine.

What Swift had done was figure a way to use special frequency lasers to create an antimatter reaction in the unstable elements he'd stolen. The nuclear fuel had been smashed together to form a superexplosion, pressed in upon itself by a stronger version of Tom's containment field.

Tom was impressed that his evil twin had

been able to create the necessary lasers and field generators from the equipment he had available. The job had required giant buss bars—foot-wide lengths of solid metal—to carry the enormous power. There were also hundreds of feet of wiring and dozens of exotic vacuum tubes. "Amazing," Tom breathed.

Thomas Swift's experiment had also been incredibly dangerous. Instead of the small setup Tom had used, his evil twin had planned to blast a one-shot escape. Either his portal would open, or most of Southern California would get blown off the map.

While Tom shook his head, staring at the screen, Dan Coster got up from the sofa, yawning.

"You've been fooling with that machine for too long," he said. "Now you're beginning to talk to it." He yawned again. "I'm heading for bed." Dan padded off to the bedroom that he and Tom were sharing.

Mandy Coster had been sitting beside her cousin on the sofa. Now she swung up her legs and lay back. Her eyes were glued to the science-fiction magazine she was reading.

Tom kept running through screens until the words blurred before his eyes. At last, he leaned back with a sigh. So did Mandy.

Embarrassed, they grinned at each other.

"Finish the story?" Tom asked.

She nodded. "Yup. The hero managed to rebuild his portal device using alien technology and returned to his own universe." She glanced over at the computer. "And you?"

"Thomas Swift is a brilliant guy. But he's reckless, so reckless it's scary. He figured how to create a black hole without even knowing what black holes are. I'd never have come up with his method, even if I was desperate."

Rising from his chair, Tom rubbed his tired back.

On the sofa, Mandy swung her legs down again, patting the cushion beside her. "So now you've got a way to go home?"

Tom sat on the sofa. "I don't know if it will work. According to his notes, I may not be able to go back to my own world. But I've got to try in spite of the risks."

Mandy brought her knees up to her chin, clasping her arms around her shins. She glanced over at Tom. "What's it really like in the universe next door?" she asked.

Tom leaned back on the cushions, relaxing. He glanced over at her. "Different," he said.

She gave him a look. "I could guess *that*," she said. "Different how?"

"Just different." Tom frowned. "The main difference between this universe and the one I came from seems to be that here my father died. It's pretty weird. Dan got some history books for me. You've had the same wars, the same presidents, everything like that. But the science—well, it looks as if my dad sparked off a lot of research and discoveries that never happened here."

Tom shook his head. "It's strange to think that one man could have so much influence. I never realized that about Dad."

Mandy nodded. "It's like that Christmas movie—the one where the guy gets to see what the world would be like if he'd never existed."

"That's it, exactly." Tom smiled ruefully. "I never realized how my father—and Swift Enterprises—made life so much . . ." He searched for a word. "*Easier* for so many people. I never told Dan that both his parents are still alive in my universe. His dad works for mine, and his mother—well, she got the treatment she needed. And Dan himself, well, he's a wise guy, but he's not quite so, so . . ."

"Dangerous." Mandy filled in the word.

They sat in silence for a moment, while she studied Tom's face. "You know me in that other universe, too," Mandy finally said softly. "What am I like?"

"Well, uh, you go to Central Hills High, with Dan and Rick Cantwell and me. You're a smart student, popular. People asked you to try out for the cheerleaders, but you didn't. You're funny, smart, and—and real nice." Tom could feel his face turning pink as he tried to come up with more things to say about the Mandy Coster he knew. He touched the magazine lying between them on the sofa. "You read a lot of science fiction."

Tom stole a glance. Mandy seemed softer, almost wistful. In spite of the tight cutoffs and tank top, she suddenly looked so similar to *his* Mandy that Tom's heart ached.

Then he realized Mandy was staring at him. "You like her, don't you?" she asked.

Tom's face went from pink to red. "We're friends."

"No, you *really* like her. I could see it in your eyes just now. Does she like you? Was she there when you did this experiment?"

"Well, yes. I mean, yes, she was there. I wanted—mmmmph!"

Tom didn't know quite how it happened. One second, Mandy was sitting there, grinning wickedly as he floundered. The next thing he knew, she had just about tackled him, putting a lip-lock on him. The Mandy from *his* world never kissed like that!

They tumbled together on the sofa. Then Mandy pulled back for air, giggling. Tom jumped to his feet, gulped, and headed for the window to hide his confusion.

Mandy followed him, leaning into his back. "Hey, it wasn't that bad, was it?" She put her arms around him.

"It was fine, Mandy." Tom's voice was as

tense as his body. "But we've got other problems. Where are all those headlights coming from? There's *never* any night traffic on that road."

"Maybe—" Mandy began.

"Maybe nothing," Tom said. "Look at all those cars by the registration office—big, fast, not too recognizable."

"Unmarked cars," Mandy said hoarsely. "Looks like the law's tracked you down."

Tom glanced at Mandy. "The question is, what do we do about it?"

"Well, it's a cinch that the cops will be watching the front door. Probably the car, too." Mandy frowned. "In fact, we shouldn't bet that they haven't surrounded the whole cabin."

"We have one bit of luck," Tom said. "The guys out there haven't moved yet. They're waiting for something before they kick down the door. That gives us a chance to get out of here, if we can distract them."

He turned to Mandy. "Get Dan, then go into the bathroom and turn on the shower. If anybody's listening out there, we want them to think that everything's normal in here."

Mandy headed for Dan's room. A moment later, her cousin came out, rubbing his eyes. "What's going on? I just zonked out—"

"Wearing your outdoor clothes?" Tom asked.

Dan glanced down. "Hey, I was bushed."

"Forget that." Tom explained their problem. "Did you move the leftover stuff from the car-painting job—the paints, the solvents—out of the bedroom?"

Dan looked a little sheepish. "I threw out the rags when you complained about the smell. But the cans and things, well . . ."

"Good," Tom said. "That means we have the start of an incendiary bomb. Have you got a pack of matches?"

"Matches?" Dan began digging through his pockets, then stopped. "Incendiary—that means a firebomb. You're going to open the solvent cans and throw a match in?"

Tom found a motel matchbook and started scraping the match heads into an ashtray with his pocketknife. He glanced up. "Nope. We need a time-delay fuse, and I think we've got the makings for one."

He handed the ashtray to Dan. "You keep scraping. I'll get the stuff from the bedroom."

Dan found another pack of matches and started scraping. As he worked, he heard the shower from the bathroom, and a muffled crack from the room where Tom had gone.

Tom came back carrying the remains of the motel clock radio. The clock was still okay, but the radio had been smashed open. Tom was pulling wires out, smiling. "Okay. Here's our timer. Are you done with the matches?"

"This is all we've got." Dan showed Tom the contents of the ashtray. "Enough?"

"It'll have to do." Tom put the radio down. "Now let's move the sofa over to the door."

"To keep the cops out?"

"No, to keep their attention. That's what we're going to set on fire."

Mandy joined in, helping to shift the sofa. "Let's get the solvent cans," Tom said. "And we'll need a plastic cup from the bathroom."

In moments, Tom had spattered the sofa with flammable liquid, leaving the rest of the can sitting in a big puddle of solvent. He soaked the drapes by the windows, too.

"Okay, now. We've got a power source—the radio; flash powder—match scrapings; and an accelerant—the solvent. By setting the alarm, I've got my timer. When the alarm goes off, it will send a spark to the flash powder and ignite the solvent."

"Then the sofa will burn," Mandy said.

Tom grinned. "And if that doesn't get the cops' attention, *nothing* will." He set the alarm. "Okay, we've got five minutes. Let's get moving."

Mandy's bedroom was in the rear of the cabin. Its lights were off, and it faced away from the motel office. Tom eased the window open. "Straight out of here," he whispered to Mandy. "Get into the underbrush and work your way back over to the Cord."

Mandy nodded, then slipped out the window. Bent low, she scurried for the brush. Nobody stopped her.

Tom tapped Dan on the back. "You next."

Dan took off, slinking into the darkness. But Tom didn't take off after him. He went back to the living room, packing Thomas Swift's computer into its case. Then, with a reluctant look around the cabin he was about to destroy, he slipped out the window.

Burdened with the extra sixty pounds, Tom staggered off. He had to take a much more difficult route to get to the car. Before he got there, though, a hand appeared from behind a bush, catching him in the chest.

"We're stuck," Dan's voice whispered in his ear. "They've got guys on the car."

Tom caught sight of the two shadowy forms standing near the Cord. One of them was looking at a wristwatch. "What's the holdup?" he asked in a whiny voice.

A deeper voice answered, "The big boss wants to be in on the kill. That Kennedy guy has been after Swift for three years—ever since the kid came up with the undetectable substitute ink for counterfeiting."

The man with the whiny voice said, "I hear he nearly caught him in that A-bomb case."

The deeper voice turned grim. "He was a little too eager, bursting into a room to nail the kid. Instead, the kid nearly nailed him with a booby trap. It should have killed Kennedy, but he managed to pull back. So he wound up with scars all over his face, instead. No wonder he wants that kid."

The kid they wanted—or rather, his twin—stood a mere ten feet away, counting down.

Now! Tom Swift looked up. All of a sudden, the front windows of the cabin grew much brighter.

Then came a muffled thump, then a whoosh, and the whole cabin burst into flames.

9

GENIUS. PURE GENIUS." THOMAS SWIFT'S intense blue eyes glittered as he looked over the wreckage in the experiment vault.

He stood by one of the walls, examining the remains of a half-melted laser. "Look at this emitter. It's been altered to discharge subatomic particles."

"I don't know what's so impressive about that, Tom. It's the same design your dad uses in the fusion reactor," Rick said. "You're acting like you've never seen this stuff before in your life."

"That's *Thomas*," Tom's evil twin snapped with a frown.

"Right, right." Rick raised his hands apologetically. "I forgot."

"Well, remember." Thomas turned his back on Rick, still examining the laser. "So the old man designed this himself, did he?" His voice fell, as if he were speaking to himself. "Hmmph. He's smarter than I—"

He checked himself, glancing back at Rick. "He's smarter than *anyone* I know."

Rick just shook his head. Tom must have taken some knock on the head. He was beginning to sound as if he had a few screws loose.

Kneeling by one of the piles of debris, Rick poked around. "Why are we hanging around here, anyway? This stuff is completely trashed. In this entire room, there's nothing worth saving—"

"Circuit Board One intact," a voice interrupted. Both boys turned to the corner. Rob and Orb were standing beside a housing that had broken open. The tall robot had a panel open, with wires leading into the out-of-commission equipment.

Rick realized there was a faint hum coming from Orb.

"Circuit Board Two intact," Orb reported. The robot's mild voice was quiet for a moment. "I believe we should run general diagnostics on this apparatus. It seems we can salvage the entire piece."

"Nothing worth saving?" Thomas Swift asked smugly.

"Tom . . . Thomas," Rick quickly amended.

82

"What are you trying to do here? First you lock yourself away, then all you want to do is hang out where—"

He was about to say, "where you seem to have lost your mind." But Rick thought better of that. "Um, where you had your terrible accident. I don't think it's healthy."

All of a sudden, a big smile appeared on Thomas's face. "Sorry, old buddy. I was just distracted by all this hardware. It really blows me away. To tell you the truth, I didn't know that I could design this. It's really awesome."

He raised a hand, his smile getting a little embarrassed. "Hey, I'm not bragging or anything. I really don't remember designing this."

Rick nodded, feeling embarrassed, too. Maybe he wasn't being fair, getting on Tom's case. After all, he couldn't blame Tom for having amnesia.

He glanced over at his friend, who was examining a video camera that had been mounted on the wall. It had been torn off, then smashed in the explosions. The film cassette was broken open, and the tape was coiled all over the place. Some was burned. All was lost.

"You know, none of the cameras in the vault survived, so we don't have a record of the experiment." Thomas looked intently at Rick. "What *really* happened?"

"I'm not sure," Rick admitted. "You were trying to make a black hole, and I think you really did it. At least, when the two lasers blasted into each other, weird stuff began to happen."

He went on to describe the creepy blue-black glow that had appeared, how it grew, and how Tom had gone to cut the power.

"Then we think you stumbled, fell into the negative light—and everything blew up." Rick shook his head. "It's not something I'd like to see again soon. I'm glad your father is shutting this project down until they can figure out what went wrong."

Rick realized that Thomas was already ignoring him. His fickle friend was over talking with Rob.

Rick could hardly make out Thomas's voice over the sound of Orb's humming. "So, you're saying that these lasers are standard equipment—we could get replacements set up right away."

"You know, pulling that kind of trick is something *I'd* do," Rick said, coming over. "I hope you're not thinking about trying another shot at that experiment."

Thomas gave him another of those brilliant but not-quite-right smiles. "No way, pal. I think I've learned my lesson. No new experiments until I remember the last one, that's my motto."

He gave Rick a carefully disinterested look. "Do you think this was the most dangerous experiment I ever did?"

Rick gave an embarrassed shrug. "Well, I don't know. You've tried some pretty crazy stuff over the years. But this is the first time you tried to fool around with the universe."

Thomas Swift nodded. "Hey, my dad used to get into some real daredevil stuff. Rockets that blew up—even with my mom around." His face became a little cold.

"Does Dad still pull stunts like that?" Thomas asked. "How about my sister . . ." He hesitated for a second, as if he had to remember her name. "Sandra. Does she get up to—"

"Hey, she must have heard you thinking about her," Rick said loudly. "Here's Sandra now!"

He was really beginning to wonder what the story was with his best friend. Obviously, nobody had told Tom that Rick and Sandra had been going out lately. What sort of death-defying stunts was Tom expecting to hear about?

"Here's the mad scientist," Sandra said with a grin. Her long blond hair was pulled back in a ponytail, and she wore a beach wrap over a lime-green bathing suit. Running shoes protected her feet from the wreckage on the floor. With her was Dan Coster, wearing a pair of wildly colored jams.

"Hey, Tom-Tom," he said. "How about we head for the beach and catch some rays?"

"You've been hanging around indoors too much lately," Sandra added. "I think some sun and surf would do you good."

Thomas Swift didn't even look up from the ruins of the containment field generator. "Thanks, but I want to see how much of this stuff we can save. I mean, you can guess how I feel about turning all this equipment into garbage."

Sandra gave him a look. "That's the first time I've ever heard you worrying about *that*," she said.

Thomas still didn't look up.

Hands on her hips, Sandra glared at the boy she thought was her brother. "Okay," she said, annoyed. "I can see I'll have to bring in the heavy artillery."

Turning toward the entrance to the bunker, Sandra raised her voice. "Hey, Mandy!" she yelled. "Come on in here!"

"Mandy is trying out a new bathing suit today—and it's pretty hot," Dan said.

Sandra grinned. "If this doesn't make you want to come along, I'm going to have to talk to your doctors, Tom."

"That's *Thomas!*" he corrected her.

Mandy Coster stepped into the debris-filled vault, looking a little embarrassed. Although she was also wearing a beach wrap, they could see that her new suit was a black bikini.

"Uh, hi, Thomas." She had heard the way Tom had spoken to his sister.

"Better bring along lots of suntan oil." Dan nudged Thomas with his elbow. "You don't want Mandy to get sunburned—do you?"

Thomas barely spared a glance from the equipment he was helping to test.

Mandy stood where she was, mortified. "I said it wouldn't work," she whispered to Sandra.

Rick stared at his friend in shock. "Maybe we *should* talk to the doctors," he suggested, only half-joking.

Thomas Swift finally turned away from the containment field generator. His face was that of a stranger—an angry stranger.

"Look," he said, his voice icy. "I've got more important things to do than waste my time at the beach with a bunch of snotty-nosed vics—"

He realized they were staring at him and abruptly shut up. "Can't you guys just let me get better my own way?" He didn't even look at them, turning back to the broken equipment.

Mandy and Sandra shared stricken glances. "Um, Rick, would you like to come?" Sandra finally asked.

"Nah. You guys go alone. I'll stay here and help Tom—Thomas—out." Rick tried to smile, but his face felt a little funny. "You guys just do us a favor—promise you won't let some beach bums pick you up."

The girls weren't laughing as they and Dan hurriedly left the bunker. Neither was Rick. He was staring at Thomas Swift, a cloud of suspicion settling around his face.

Snotty-nosed vics. That's what Tom had called the kids on the beach. Rick knew what "vic" was—it was street talk, criminal slang for "victim." What was going on with his friend?

"Hey, Rick," Thomas called over. "There's a power grid next to you. Could you just pick that up?"

Rick bent to get the piece of equipment, hoping that Tom hadn't caught the look on his face.

Thomas Swift had. As Rick touched the exposed circuitry, Thomas whispered something to Orb. A panel opened, and wires flew out.

Rick didn't know what happened. All of a sudden a surge of power was flashing through the power grid. He shuddered from the sudden shock, unable to control his muscles, to open his hands and escape.

"T-T-T-Tom!" he managed to get out.

Then the power grid exploded.

10

A WILD ERUPTION OF FLAME BURST FROM THE windows and doors of the motel cabin. The pair of guards standing by Tom Swift's car stared, almost hypnotized by the sudden glare.

Tom and Dan pounced immediately, grabbing the two police officers before they could call for help. Dan whipped his target around and decked him with a roundhouse right. Tom got a choke hold on his man. Although the man thrashed wildly, he couldn't escape the forearm at his throat. In moments he, too, lay unconscious.

Dan grinned, rubbing his left hand over a set of aching knuckles. "Looks like we're done here."

Tom nodded. "Let's get moving."

They stowed the computer behind the seat and piled into the car. Police and official-looking types were converging on the burning cabin. No one seemed to be paying attention as the long, repainted Cord eased into motion.

Tom steered past the group of unmarked cars, got on the road, and headed east. Soon they hooked up with the interstate, heading northeast.

Dan squinted at a sign that read, Las Vegas—110 Miles.

"I figured we were heading for L.A. after the fire drill you set up back there," he said. "With all the guys beating the bushes for you, Swift, I thought you'd want someplace with lots of people to hide among."

He grinned. "Not that Vegas isn't okay, mind you. Maybe I can bluff my way in to play at the blackjack tables—"

"Don't bet on it," Tom said wearily. He glanced over at Dan. "How'd you like a chance to drive for a while?"

"Like to drive this machine?" Dan flexed his fingers, eager to get behind the wheel. "Do bears bear? Do bees bee?"

Tom pulled the Cord over to the shoulder, then switched places with Dan. "Just keep heading for Vegas. Don't break the speed limit or call attention to us. If you can find us a place to hole up north of town, grab it."

"What are you going to be doing?" Mandy asked.

"A lot of heavy thinking," Tom answered. "And then I want to catch some Zs. There's going to be a busy day ahead."

Tom cried out in his sleep. "Trapped! No! I don't want to be stuck here."

Dan shook his head as he braked outside a small motel north of Las Vegas. "I don't know what the story is, but whenever he closes his eyes, he has nightmares."

Gently, Mandy shook Tom awake. "You okay?"

His eyes were a little wild as they opened. "Got to get back," he muttered. Then he realized where they were. "Mandy, why don't you register for us?" Tom grimaced. "Let's hope there's no APB out on our new, improved car."

Dan had turned the car from gray to a quiet dark green, but Tom was worried that the Cord Speedster's rakish lines would give them away.

He turned to Mandy. "Try to give the desk clerk the idea that you lost a bundle in Vegas and decided to head home to Montana early."

"Don't you think he's going to get suspicious when he sees our California plates?" Dan asked.

"Thomas Swift had a stash of license plates

hidden under the carpeting in the trunk,"
Tom said. "I found them when we were getting ready for the painting job and noticed
that there's one from Montana in the collec-
tion. We'll just switch plates and see how
good an actress Mandy is."

Apparently, the desk clerk swallowed Mandy's story hook, line, and sinker. Within
minutes of Mandy's getting the keys to a
cabin, they were turning in.

The police weren't the only ones who'd
been caught by surprise when flames burst
out of Tom Swift's last hideout. As the place
exploded, a nondescript station wagon was
coming down the road. One look at the fire
and the assembled unmarked cars, and the
wagon screeched into a U-turn.

"He must have been there, just like we
heard." George Finn's hands were white on
the steering wheel. "Otherwise, why are all
these cops hanging around out there?"

"Do you think they caught him?" Len Dinwiddie knelt on the front seat, staring back
through the rear windshield. "Did they set
that house on fire, or"—he thought for a
moment—"do you think *he* did?" From the
way Dinwiddie said the word, there was no
doubt who he was talking about.

"I don't know, Len, but I wasn't going to
hang around and ask." Finn gave a deep sigh.

"If the cops did catch—or kill—the boss . . ." For a second, he sounded almost hopeful. "I guess we'll hear about it soon enough."

His face grew even glummer than usual. "If not, I guess the radio will be full of that, too." He sighed. "And then, we'll have to track him down again."

Early the next morning, Mandy padded out into the cabin's living room. Tom was already up, staring at the computer monitor.

"Whatcha doing?" Mandy asked, yawning.

"Couldn't sleep—those dreams again." Tom shook his head. "So I've been figuring how to get home. First stop, the Desert Range atomic reactor." He patted the computer monitor. "Thomas Swift has detailed plans of the place in here."

Mandy stared. "What do we want with an atomic reactor?"

"Fuel. Thomas used the stuff he got from the terrorists to open his dimensional portal. So I have to get some of my own if I'm going to get home." Tom looked at the surprised expression on Mandy's face. "I *need* to go home. Those dreams are telling me something. I don't like hunches, but I'm sure something bad is going on. I have to get back there . . . if I can." His face grew grim. "And I'm running out of time."

"Sure you're not just lonely for your girl-friend?"

Tom's face softened as he realized Mandy was teasing him. "Nah. If it was just that, I think I could find a nice girl here. I've just got this weird feeling. It says I'd better go back."

Mandy came over to the table and leaned over Tom's shoulder so she could see the computer screen. "Okay, so what's the plan?"

"First, we hit a few electronic supply places. I need some equipment for my alter ego's space-warp gizmo. Then we'll be ready to rebuild it as soon as I get the fuel."

By the time Dan woke up, Tom and Mandy had already gotten the scientific supplies. Then they bought gear for the attempt on the nuclear plant. They were out of town by four o'clock, setting off on the three-hour drive to the Desert Range site.

The reactor was set on a salt flat in the middle of nowhere. Three heavy chain-link fences surrounded the installation. Each of them was posted with warnings and No Trespassing signs.

"Real friendly-looking place," Dan commented. They were checking out the reactor from a hilly ridge about two miles away. The setting sun was painting the desert a vivid orange.

"I don't see how we can sneak up on that joint—not with all that flat land around it," Mandy said.

"It's not as flat as it looks." Tom's eyes were glued to a pair of binoculars. For the last hour, he'd been monitoring the guards' routine. The movements of the uniformed men matched exactly the data in Thomas Swift's computer.

Tom finally looked away from the gates. "There's a streambed that nearly cuts past the northeast corner of the outer fence. It will be dry this time of year. We can use it for cover, drive as close as we can, then take the rest of the way on foot."

A little while after full dark, they were picking their way along a narrow, pebble-floored gully. Their car was parked about a half-mile behind them, where the empty streambed had finally gotten too tight to drive through.

"This should be about as close as we can get." Tom scrambled to the top of the gully wall and peered south. Just a little way off was the corner of the first fence. "Come on."

They all climbed out of the little canyon, heading for the fence. "The map shows the gates on the other side," Mandy said.

"We're making our own entrance," Dan said with a grin. He pulled a heavy-duty pair of wire-cutters from the pack on his back.

Soon they were through the fences and

heading for the main reactor building. "No noise once we're inside," Tom said in a low whisper. "And stay with me. Thomas Swift marked one safe route into the area we want."

Following his evil twin's plans, Tom led Mandy and Dan into the building and down a corridor to a tiny room. The door was unlocked. "Good," said Tom, stuffing the map into his pocket.

The room they had stepped into was barely large enough to hold the three of them. Its main feature was a control panel with several clumsy-looking joysticks facing a thick lead-glass window. On the other side of the window lay the reactor core.

Tom stepped to the panel, grasped a pair of the joysticks, and moved them tentatively.

In the room beyond the window, a pair of long, jointed metal arms began to move.

"What are those?" Dan asked, staring.

"They're called waldoes," Tom said, still getting the feel of the controls. His thumb pressed a button at the top of one of the right-hand joysticks. Inside the reactor room, the three-pincer grapple at the end of the right-hand arm clacked together.

"You might call them artificial hands," Tom went on. Now he had the hang of the controls. "They're very useful when you have to do work in dangerous environments." He grinned at Dan. "Like picking up slugs of radioactive material and sticking them into carrying cases."

A set of lead-lined yellow boxes was already in the reactor room. Each was stenciled with the message Warning—Radioactive Material.

Tom maneuvered one of the robot arms over to a box, dipped it down, and used the grapples to pull open the top.

"Okay, here we go," he said, peering into the four empty slots in the box.

He sent the waldoes over to a pigeonholed bin marked Breeder Reactor—Fuel Slugs, and started poking the robot arms inside. After a couple of false starts, he withdrew the grapple, which now clutched a three-inch long lead-lined rod. Jockeying the controls back and forth, he jerkily managed to bring the rod to the carrying case and slip it into one of the slots.

"One down," Tom breathed.

"It's sort of like that game in the arcades, where you dig around with a robot arm to get a good prize," Mandy said.

"Don't remind me," Tom said, already moving a second slug. "Whenever I pop quarters into that, I always wind up with a piece of junk. Gotcha!"

He slipped the second slug in place.

The job got harder as he went along, since there were fewer slots to fill and his movements had to be more precise. Tom tried to hurry the job along, and nearly dropped the third slug of nuclear fuel.

"Whoa!" he said as the fuel rod began slipping through the fingers of the grapple. Tom quickly brought the other arm over and caught the slug before it fell.

"Great catch, huh, Dan? Dan?" Mandy glanced at her cousin, but he wasn't there. All she saw was the open door into the corridor they'd come down.

Mandy turned her attention back to the spectacle of Tom teasing the fuel rod into the carrying case. It caught on the corner of the case, teetered for a moment, and finally slid home.

"Last one," Tom said. He plucked one more fuel slug from its pigeonhole and started maneuvering it. With only one slot left, he had quite a struggle lining up the rod.

At last, the slug was directly over the slot. Tom released the grapples, and the rod dropped home.

In the next instant a siren began to wail.

Tom jumped back from the controls. "What did I do?" he asked.

"Not you—Dan." Mandy's face looked scared, but she was angry, too.

"That fool's just set off an alarm."

11

THOMAS SWIFT STOOD OVER THE STILL FORM of Rick Cantwell. The young genius's face was a study in cold calculation.

He was busily balancing factors in his head, as if he were working out a difficult equation. Cantwell had turned down the offer to go to the beach, just so he could keep an eye on him. He'd actually looked suspicious. Thomas Swift cursed himself for letting his tongue slip. But who would have thought that a straight would know anything about street language?

It's too late now, he reminded himself. What are you going to do with this guy? That's the question. From now on he'll be watching me. Maybe it's better to silence his suspicions right away—permanently.

Rick Cantwell had fallen across another power grid. It would be so easy—just power the equipment up for a moment or two. The second set of shocks would probably do the job.

Abruptly, Thomas Swift shook his head. No. It wouldn't do for Cantwell to die—yet. It wouldn't do to have a fatal accident happen so soon before the ones he was planning.

"Orb," he said, turning to the round robot on the floor, "call the rescue team. And get the head technician down here, too.'"

Swift pointed at the unconscious Rick Cantwell. "Rob, pick him up and bring him to the door."

The robot scooped up Rick's limp form and carried him through the blast shields. From the distance, Thomas Swift heard a siren approaching—the rescue team ambulance, he realized.

"Rob!" he called after the robot. "Don't step outside."

Thomas Swift dashed along the open sections of the vault floor, leaping over smaller piles of debris. He reached Rob and the outer doors just as the rescue wagon pulled up.

"Quick. Give him to me," Swift said, taking Rick from the robot's arms.

When Rick Cantwell emerged from the bunker, he was cradled in Thomas Swift's arms.

Thomas staggered out, his face a picture of grief and worry.

"My friend has been hurt!" he cried, voice shaking. "Electrical shock. Get him to the hospital right away!"

The rescue team charged forward to take Rick.

Thomas Swift watched them set to work. Outwardly, he seemed very anxious. Inside, he was highly pleased. Step one, he told himself.

He saw a van come screaming up to the bunker. A man in a white lab coat flung himself from behind the wheel and ran for the doors. Inwardly, Thomas Swift smiled. Now for step two.

"Walton," he yelled, getting the man's name from the ID card clipped to his lab coat lapel. "I thought you'd cut all power to this bunker, but my friend just got a severe electrical shock. How do you explain that?"

"M-Mister Swift—sir," Walton stammered. "I—I don't know."

"Well, you're going to find out." Thomas Swift spit out the words in a tough tone of voice. "Between now and this evening, your crew is going to remove all the equipment in the bunker—it's obviously unsafe—and replace it. *Every* piece, get it? Rob will provide you with plans."

Walton blanched. "The containment field

generator? The special laser emitters? We'll have to close down one of the fusion banks—"

"I don't care what it takes," Thomas snapped, cutting him off. "Just do it. I believe I've isolated what went wrong with this experiment, and I expect that my father and I will be checking it out tonight."

"You and your father will be working together?" Walton said, impressed. "I don't think you've done that in years. I mean, you usually don't bring in—"

"This is hardly a usual case," Thomas Swift said abruptly. "As for my father, let's just say I had a potent convincer."

He stalked to the door of the bunker. "Rob! Get Orb and come with me!"

In a moment, the tall, gleaming robot appeared, carrying the silver, spherical robot brain under its arm.

"The bunker is now empty." Thomas Swift turned to Walton with a curt jerk of his head. "Get to work!"

Thomas set off across the Swift Enterprises grounds on foot, trailed by the two robots. He cut across the lawn, heading for the administration building and his lab. Just as they came through the lab door, Rob spoke up.

"It's time," the robot said. "The chemicals you put in the mixer have been blending exactly an hour and a half."

"Good." Thomas Swift went over to the

automatic mixer and turned it off. The tiny blades whirring in the laboratory flask stopped moving. Thomas poured the clear liquid in the flask into a test tube, put a stopper in the top, then placed the vial in his breast pocket.

"That's done," he said. "Now, Rob, I want you to clean this flask very carefully, then destroy it." The smile on Thomas Swift's face was not very nice as he patted the vial in his pocket.

"Rob," he said, as his robot started washing out the lab flask, "if I showed you a handwriting sample, could you reproduce it—exactly?"

"Of course." Rob took the now-clean flask over to a lab table, shattered it, then began grinding the remaining fragments.

"Good." Thomas Swift sifted through some papers on another table. When he came back to Rob, the robot had reduced the flask to a pile of tiny glass splinters.

"Just bury them somewhere," Thomas Swift ordered. "But first . . ." He shoved a piece of paper in front of Rob's photocell eyes, pointing. "This is the handwriting sample I want you to copy." He put a piece of paper on the table. "And this is what I want you to copy it onto."

Rob's eyes glittered as he looked at the sample. "This is your father's signature." The robot turned to the paper. "And this is an authorization to use the particle accelerator."

"That's right. I want to be ready to reduplicate my experiment tonight, but I don't want to bother Dad with the details."

Rob was silent for a long moment. "This is forgery. I am not—"

Thomas Swift looked bored. "We don't have to go through this again, do we? I've reprogrammed you so that my orders take priority over all other restrictions."

"Yes." Rob's voice sounded a little faint.

"Fine. Here's a pen. Get to work, then deliver the authorization to whoever runs the particle accelerator." Thomas Swift went back to his worktable and sat there, reading another science book. "And, Rob?" he said, glancing over his shoulder.

The robot had already finished the forgery, and was heading to the door. Now it stopped. "Yes, Thomas?"

"Remind me to go to the hospital around midafternoon. It would look good for me to be inquiring how my poor friend Rick Cantwell is doing." With a contemptuous grin, Thomas Swift went back to his book.

Supper at the Swift house was usually a cheerful time, with conversation, jokes, and lots of good food. When Thomas came to the table this evening, however, he immediately picked up on the tense atmosphere. Sandra Swift gave her brother a sidelong glance as he sat down. Mrs. Swift busied herself serving food, not looking at him at all. Tom senior sat at his plate with a frown, tapping his fingers ominously on the table.

"Dr. Thorndyke says you were at the hospital this afternoon," Mr. Swift said as Thomas began serving himself.

"Oh, right. I bumped into him while I was visiting Rick. I guess you heard about the accident in the bunker."

"I'm concerned for Rick, but I'm more concerned for you, Tom."

"That's Thomas."

"All, right—Thomas." Mr. Swift's face was red as he took a sip of lemonade. "The doctor hasn't seen you since you came home after the accident. He wanted to examine you, and you refused. Why?"

"I'm working on something, and I didn't want to lose time right now. If it will make the doctor happy, I'll see him tomorrow. Okay?"

Mrs. Swift sipped some lemonade. "I understand the doctor was very upset— Thomas. He seems to think you brushed him off."

"Mom, I've had a lot on my mind. If I hurt the doctor's feelings, I'll do my best to make it up to him. What do you think—will *two* visits do the job?"

Sandra gulped her lemonade and stared at Tom with disbelieving eyes.

Now Mr. Swift was speaking again, very angrily. "I cut you some slack after the accident, but no one takes advantage of me. What's this I heard from Walton about you ordering him to rebuild your experimental equipment? He had to take an emitter off-line in the fusion plant to do the job."

"Right. I got the word just a little while ago that he'd finished the job."

Tom senior nodded. "I know. He reported the same thing to me because he thought that *I* was going to be doing an experiment there tonight. What are you up to in that bunker, Tom? I can tell you one thing. There'll be no esperiments . . . experimenz . . ." Mr. Swift looked a little surprised at his lapse. "We won't be doing any more work there until we can do it snavely . . . safely."

There was a clatter at the table as Sandra suddenly fell face-forward into her plate.

"S-S-Sanda," Mrs. Swift slurred. "Waz wrong?" She tried to get up from her seat, swayed, then collapsed herself.

"S'matter, here?" Mr. Swift's eyes were glazed as he gripped the edge of the table. For a moment, they cleared again, and he glared at Thomas Swift. "You—" he began, forcing himself upright. But his eyes lost their focus. Then Tom senior fell to the floor, unconscious.

Thomas Swift reached into his pocket, taking out a test tube. He glanced from the now-empty vial to the lemonade pitcher, smiling evilly. His chemical mixture had worked perfectly.

Pushing aside his untouched meal, Thomas Swift went over to stand above the man who thought he was his father. "Don't be concerned about me, Pops," he told the unconscious figure. "In fact, none of you will have to worry about anything, ever again."

His smile became more and more twisted.

"And I won't have to worry about anyone stopping me from taking over Swift Enterprises."

12

THE SCREAMING ALARMS FROZE TOM AND Mandy for a second. Then, while the hoots and sirens continued, Tom grabbed for the waldo controls. His first few tries at using the robot arms to close the carrying case full of nuclear fuel were fumbled through his haste.

"One last try," he said through gritted teeth. Taking a deep breath, he willed his hands to be steady. Carefully manipulating the controls, he got the box closed, sealed, and placed in the connecting door between the reactor and the room he was in.

The setup was like a spaceship airlock. The hatch in the control room opened only when the hatch in the reactor room was closed. As they waited for the two doors to cycle, Mandy fidgeted nervously by the entrance to the corridor.

"C'mon, Swift!" she hissed. "There have to be guards around here. Sooner or later they're gonna get off their coffee break and check this room out." She frowned at Tom. "And I'd rather not be here when they come."

"Just another couple of seconds," Tom begged. "If you hear them coming, run for it yourself."

Mandy gave him a look. "Yeah, right, Tom. Like I'd really leave you behind."

Hearing Mandy say that made Tom feel good, but there was no time to talk just then. At long last the inner door was opening. Tom reached into the lock and grabbed the sealed box of fuel.

Tom grunted as he picked the box up. "Great," he muttered, hefting it. "Heavy elements and lead shielding. First that stupid computer, now this. Don't I ever get something *light* to haul on this misadventure?"

"Right now, I think you'd better haul your butt out of here," Mandy cut in. "I'll be right behind you. There's somebody coming down the hallway outside."

They jumped into the corridor, determined not to be trapped in the control room. But Tom and Mandy didn't have to fight or flee. They knew the red-faced figure running down the hall.

"Dan!" Mandy yelled at her cousin. "You stupid—"

"Hey, guys, what can I say?" Dan panted as he came up to them. "I only meant to take a peek into that stupid office. You'd think I committed a federal offense or something."

"Dan, just breaking into a reactor is a federal offense," Tom snapped as they started down the hallway.

"Oh, yeah," Dan muttered. "Right."

Army-issue boots clattered on the concrete floors. "They can't have gotten this far, Sarge," a nervous voice boomed from around the corner. "I mean, this is the center of the installation."

Tom, Mandy, and Dan looked at one another, then took off like deer in the opposite direction.

"Split up," Tom whispered. "Maybe one of us can get away. Whoever reaches the car first, uses it."

"Gotcha." Dan darted down an intersecting hallway and disappeared.

Mandy just shook her head and stayed with Tom. "That was stupid, you know," she told him in an angry whisper. "Dan isn't lugging half a ton as he runs. He'll get to the Cord first, and we'll be left sucking car exhaust."

"I said it so *you* could get away, Mandy."

They were still running along the main corridor, and Tom was beginning to feel the weight of the fuel case in his shoulders and arms.

"Oh, swell. You're being noble." Mandy was trying to sound annoyed, but there was something else shining in her eyes.

"I don't know how anybody could mistake you for Thomas Swift," she finally said.

A door ahead of them opened, and a technician in a white coverall backed out.

"Definitely not a core meltdown," he was saying to somebody in the room. "That was the intruder alert, for sure. I thought you guys had beefed up security after Thomas Swift and those terrorists hit that reactor in Arizona—"

The man turned, and his eyes bugged out as he caught sight of the two fugitives.

"Herbie! Come quick! It-it's Thomas Swift!"

The door flew open, and out stepped a man in combat fatigues. He was built on the lines of a Mack truck, and he was armed with an M-16 rifle.

"Run, Mandy," Tom said, pushing her ahead of him down the branching corridor. He crashed into her from behind and then saw why she'd stopped. The corridor ended in a big set of double doors marked Emergency Exit.

"If this isn't an emergency, I don't know what is," Tom said. He and Mandy dashed down the short corridor.

Behind them, they heard the echo of their

pursuer's boots. The guard must be a real glory-hound, Tom thought. He hasn't called anybody else in—must want to catch us all by himself. Tom refused to look back to see if the guy had cleared the corner. All of Tom's attention was on reaching the emergency exit.

A hoarse voice behind them bellowed, "All right, you two—freeze!" as Tom and Mandy hit the panic bar on the door. They tumbled into the darkness outside, and a warning shot whizzed between them.

Tom tripped over something on the ground and lurched desperately, struggling to stay on his feet. His arm felt as if it were about to be torn off at the shoulder by the carrying case, but no way was he letting go of his ticket out. Losing the fuel rods would doom him as surely as the guard's bullets.

He tried to stumble out of the shaft of light thrown from the door, but now there was a new shadow blocking it. The guard came storming out, his M-16 at the ready. "No more warning shots, Swift," the man snarled. "One funny move, and I blow you away."

Tom whipped around, facing the angry guard. He could see a silhouette against the light, but nothing else. The indoor light was blinding him. Although Tom couldn't make out the guard's face, he could imagine it. Big, square, tough, furious—the guy probably spent his spare time pumping iron and wolfing steroids.

"Now drop that box," the guard ordered.

Tom's hand instinctively tightened on the case's handle. "N-no," he said.

The rifle came up. "Last warning."

Tom stood where he was, unmoving.

A second shadow appeared in the doorway, behind the guard. It was slimmer, with one hand upraised.

Then came a very familiar thud. Tom grinned. He'd heard that sound before.

"Ooof!" said the guard, pivoting to cover his attacker. Mandy swung again. This time the guard crumpled to the ground.

"Where did you go?" Tom asked as Mandy came running toward him.

"I came out that door and flung myself against the wall next to it," Mandy said. "That's what I thought *you* were going to do."

Tom shrugged, a little embarrassed. "Maybe that's what I would have done, if I hadn't tripped." He looked around. "At least we're out of the building. Now let's work on getting through the fence."

They made their way across the reactor grounds, darting for whatever meager cover they could find. It was like a horrible game of hide-and-seek, with them dodging squads of guards.

From the way the sergeants were yelling at

the troopers, it sounded as if the security people were in a complete panic. Serious reinforcements kept arriving. Tom could see truckloads of soldiers arriving at the main gate.

"If they find where we cut through the fence, we're dead," Mandy whispered. "They can just wait to nail us."

"Well, we can't hang around to cut a new exit," Tom whispered back. "We'll just have to take our chances."

It took them a while to work their way to the corner of the reactor compound. When they did, Tom and Mandy were amazed to see Dan crouched by the hole in the outer fence.

"He waited for us!" Mandy almost gasped in surprise.

"Looks like you owe your cousin an apology," Tom said.

They dashed for the opening in the inner fence, scrambled through, and caught up with Dan.

"Hey, cuz," Mandy said, laughing. "I'm glad I didn't bet Tom about whether you'd be here. I was sure all we'd find were your tracks. How come you hung around?"

"Oh, I had a million reasons," Dan said with a tight smile.

"And you earned every one of them." A big man in a baggy suit rose out of the gully, blocking the cut in the outer fence. In his hand was an enormous pistol. "This is a forty-four Magnum. It makes big holes, so I wouldn't move."

The moon was just rising, casting a dim radiance on the face of the man who held them captive. A silvery light glanced off the huge track of scar tissue that writhed from his temple to his chin.

"Kennedy," Tom breathed.

"You remember me. How nice." The government agent now had his gun trained on Tom. "I usually hate flying at night, but when your buddy called to report that you were knocking over this reactor, I scrambled a plane. You got away the last time he dropped a dime on you."

"The motel?" Tom said numbly.

Kennedy nodded. "Girlie," he said to Mandy, "you should have kept him occupied instead of letting him go to the window. But that's all over now. I've finally got you, Swift."

"Tom, I wasn't—" Mandy began.

"Look, I'm not—" Tom said at the same instant.

"Shut up," Kennedy said. His gun was centered on Tom's face. "They've finally issued the dead-or-alive order on you, Swift." The government man cocked his trigger.

"And frankly, I don't care how I bring you in."

THOMAS SWIFT'S ARMS AND BACK WERE TIRED.
It had been tough work, moving a family of
three from the living room to the garage. He
had already parked a Swift Enterprises equipment van there, earlier in the afternoon. After
all, it wouldn't do to have somebody notice
him lugging a bunch of limp bodies around,
would it?

Still, he was whistling a cheerful tune as he
loaded each of his victims into the van. It
would have been so much easier to use that
big robot, Rob, to do the heavy work. But that
would mean completely flushing the machine's
brain. Thomas couldn't afford any witnesses
to what he was about to do, not even mechanical ones.

The whistle died on his lips as he stared down at the three figures lined up in the back of the van. Father, mother, kid sister. The family he'd never had. Two had died in his universe, one had never been born. They'd had a good life here. Thomas could tell that, even from his short time with them. This might have been the life he'd have had, if things had gone another way in another universe.

A cold look came across the young man's face. He was used to making his own luck, and very soon, he was going to make himself rich, powerful—and alone.

All he had to do was bring the Swifts to the bunker, start up the experiment that had failed, and what had happened the last time would happen again. The equipment in the vault would blow up. This time, the control room would go up, too, and all the Swifts— well, almost—would go with it.

"A sad fluke," Thomas breathed as he covered his almost-family with a thin tarp. "The black hole got free and headed for the blast shields. They couldn't stand up to it, the controls went crazy, and everyone in the control room died. Everybody but poor Thomas Swift."

He grinned at his reflection in the rearview mirror as he slid behind the wheel of the van. "I'll be running Swift Enterprises—and then, watch out, world."

He drove carefully to the Swift Enterprises complex, obeying every traffic rule, every speed limit. The gate guard just waved him through.

Thomas pulled up at the entrance to the bunker. This was the tricky part. He couldn't bring the van inside, so he'd have to risk carrying the unconscious Swifts out in the open.

Still, the van should cover the entrance from most prying eyes. Thomas quickly moved the family members into the control room, then closed the outside doors. He sighed with relief as the heavy steel portals clanged together. Thomas moved into the experiment vault to make a few adjustments to the containment field generator. Now nobody could get in.

"Tom!"

Thomas nearly dropped the wrench he was using to open the equipment housing. He whirled around to see Harlan Ames, head of Swift security, looking at him curiously.

Then Thomas realized he could see the blast shield behind the slightly glowing figure. It was one of those crazy holograms, those 3-D picturephones the people around there used. Harlan Ames wasn't actually in the room with him.

"Sorry, Harlan," Thomas said. "You startled me."

Ames nodded. "Actually, I wanted to talk

to your father. I tried him at your house, but nobody was there. I heard you folks were trying some more testing down in the bunker, so I thought . . ."

Thomas glanced over at the control room. Mrs. Swift and Mandy were both arranged in chairs behind the blast shields, out of sight. But Mr. Swift was sprawled across a control panel and could be seen through one of the Perspex windows.

"Dad? Want to talk to Harlan?" Thomas called loudly. A little bead of sweat dripped down his face. "What? Not now?"

He pointed toward the Perspex panel. "Dad shook his head no. We're working on calibrating these controls, and I guess Dad wants to get the job done. Can we call you after the test?"

Thomas hoped that Harlan would think Tom senior was leaning across the panel, working on something. The security man shrugged. "Sure. Call me later."

The image winked out of existence, and Thomas Swift breathed a deep sigh.

"I hope I'm wrong. I really hope I'm wrong." Rick Cantwell eased his throbbing arm in its sling and glanced over at Mandy Coster. Her lips were set in a thin, worried line as she drove along the road to the Swift Enterprises complex.

"When you called me from the hospital, I thought you were crazy," she admitted. "I figured, 'Great. This stupid experiment has rattled two of my friends' brains. How could Rick honestly believe that Tom tried to kill him?'"

"I guess I should be glad that you agreed to pick me up," Rick said.

"But I still didn't believe you, not until we stopped off at Tom's house and found it empty." She shuddered. "Why would everyone disappear, leaving a half-eaten meal on the table?"

"I can't believe they were so eager to get back to the testing bunker," Rick said. "But that's what Harlan Ames told me when I called the complex. Looks like the whole family's down there for a retest of that Negative Zone equipment."

"But that doesn't make sense," Mandy complained. "I talked with Sandra today. She told me that Mr. Swift was dead set against fooling around with that experiment until they had a better idea of why it went wrong." She shook her head. "Why would he change his mind?"

"And why so suddenly that they left in the middle of dinner?" Rick's face was grim, and it wasn't from the pain in his arm. "Can you speed it up a little, Mandy? I want to see what's going on in that bunker."

"I think you should have asked Harlan Ames to send some people over to check it out," Mandy said, pushing her car closer to the speed limit.

"And how was I supposed to do that?" Rick wanted to know. "Should I have told him that Tom has gone out of his mind? That he's going to kill his entire family? I don't think that Harlan would believe me." His troubled eyes scanned the road ahead of them. "I'm not sure that I believe it myself."

"You could have told Harlan what happened this morning," Mandy said. "How Tom tried to kill you."

"I had a hard enough time convincing you just to come by and pick me up," Rick responded angrily. "Do you think Harlan Ames would go barging in on his boss just on my say-so?"

They reached the main gate of the Swift complex, and a guard stepped over to their car.

"We're going to Testing Bunker Three," Mandy told the man. "That's where Tom Swift and his father are working."

The guard waved them on.

"Well, at least people will know where we are," Rick said as they drove along the perimeter road.

The area around the bunker seemed deserted, except for a van parked in front.

"Nobody behind the wheel," Rick said, glancing at the van's windshield.

Mandy pulled her car up beyond the vehicle. "And the entrance to the bunker is open."

She hit the handle for her car door. "Come on. We won't have a better chance to snoop around."

Silently, Rick and Mandy crept toward the bunker's heavy steel gates. They were open only wide enough for one person to squeeze through, and they gave hardly any view of the control room. But the two teens could hear the hum of equipment warming up inside.

"They're doing something in there," Rick said.

"I'll tell you something they're *not* doing." Mandy looked suspicious. "Nobody's saying a word. That's all just machinery noise. Let's get inside and see what's going on."

She started to slip through the open doors, then froze in midstep.

Rick crashed into her from behind. But when he saw the scene over her shoulder, he completely understood why Mandy had stopped.

Three of the Swifts—Tom senior, his wife, and Sandra—were sprawled in seats facing the blast shield. They were breathing, but their closed eyes and lax postures showed that they were unconscious.

Mr. Swift's head was thrown back over the

top of his chair. The multicolored lights on the control panel cast a ghastly glow on his pale face.

"Where's Thomas?" Mandy asked.

She took a step down the stairway toward the room, but Rick grabbed her arm. "With luck, he's in the experiment vault. Come on. We've got to get Harlan Ames and bring him over here. When he sees this, he ought to be convinced something is wrong."

They were squeezing through the doors together when the side cargo bay on the van rolled open. Thomas Swift stood in the opening, a self-powered soldering iron in his hand.

"How lucky I had to come out here and get this," he said, switching the device on.

The tip of the soldering iron began to glow—first orange, then red-hot.

Thomas Swift pointed the iron like a sword at Mandy and Rick. "I think you know what this can do," he said flatly. "So if you don't want to get hurt, I think you should go back through the door and head down those stairs."

Mandy and Rick turned around and headed back the way they'd come.

One look at Thomas Swift's face told them he wouldn't stop at just inflicting pain.

14

STARING DOWN THE BARREL OF AGENT KEN-
nedy's gun, Tom Swift flung himself into
action. With all his strength, he jerked up the
heavy case full of isotopes, swinging it at the
man's gun hand.

The carrying case connected with Kennedy's wrist just as the gun went off. It was
close enough for powder grains to burn the
side of Tom's neck. The government man
recovered fast, bringing his gun down sharply
to clip Tom on the side of the head.

White-hot lights seemed to explode behind
Tom's eyes, and he dropped to his knees. But,
surprisingly, Mandy burst into motion, dash-
ing past Dan and running through the slit in
the security fence. In seconds, she plunged
down the little gully that hid the car. As Tom

dropped to his knees, fighting not to pass out, he heard a sound in the distance—the familiar roar of the Cord's engine starting up.

She wasn't in on it, Tom realized. At least she's getting away. He was too far gone to resist as Kennedy ripped the isotope case from him, then handcuffed his wrists behind his back.

"I'd have been totally justified in blowing you away right then." The federal agent's voice grated in Tom's ear. He hauled Tom upright and yelled for the guards. Then he lowered his voice again. "But I'd much rather see you in jail. I don't even mind that girl getting away. I've got you, Swift, and I'm going to make you suffer."

The Dry Valley County sheriff's office was small and downright primitive. It consisted of a tiny lockup with whitewashed adobe walls and iron bars that was rarely used. Beside it was an even smaller area with the sheriff's desk and a couple of chairs. However, it was the jail nearest to the Desert Range Nuclear Facility, so that's where the dangerous criminal Thomas Swift wound up for interrogation.

He'd had all his clothes confiscated, and agents searched them carefully for any hidden equipment. Now Tom sat in paper slippers and a scratchy denim shirt and jeans, perched on an uncomfortable stool, with the desk lamp shining in his face. He'd endured three grueling hours of questioning. After reading Tom his rights, Agent Kennedy had been relentless, pressing Tom for details of all sorts of crimes.

The problem was that, except for the ones he'd committed in the past few days, Tom had no idea of what his evil alter ego had done, or why.

"What was the solvent you used to weaken the bulletproof glass in the German chancellor's hotel room?" Kennedy would bark at him. "How did you gimmick the computer time-lock on the Daley State Bank vault?"

Tom could only shrug.

"Where is the loot from the Rector's jewelry heist?"

When Tom tried to tell his story about black holes and alternate universes, the federal agent cut him off. "I don't know what you're trying to pull, telling me all this garbage." Kennedy waved his arm dismissively. "There's no way on earth you're going to cop an insanity plea."

"Ask Dan Coster," Tom pleaded.

Dan was brought in, looking like the cat who caught the world's biggest canary. "Swift's been spinning quite a tale," Kennedy said.

"You mean this universe-next-door stuff?" Dan shrugged. "The reward was for turning him in, dead or alive. I didn't think you'd mind if he was loony." Greed shone in Dan's eyes. "And speaking of the reward . . ."

"The check will be here by eleven in the morning," Kennedy said. "Just do me one favor before the reporters arrive."

"What?"

"Get a haircut."

Dan sauntered off, shaking his head.

Kennedy leaned across the desk he was sitting behind and glared at Tom. "I don't think he'll make a good witness for your side. Now, what's the story on this latest caper of yours? Has the International Liberation Front made another deal with you? How much are they paying you for the bombs this time?" Kennedy's face went ugly. "You can make this a lot easier on yourself. Just tell me where you've agreed to meet those dirt-bags. You'll still get life, but it will be in a better prison."

Tom tried again. "Look, Agent Kennedy. The first time I ever saw you in my life was when you popped up with a gun by the reactor fence."

"If you'd never seen me before, how did you know my name?"

"I-I'd heard about the scars on your face from a news report. Then, when I saw you in the moonlight—well, you could be only one person."

The milky scar on Kennedy's face stood out

in ghastly contrast as the agent went red. "You sure have nerve, telling me that story when *you're* the reason I've got these scars. I'll never live a normal life again, thanks to you. It takes everything I've got not to pound you to a bloody pulp. And you try egging me on."

The fed took a deep breath, then relaxed his hands, leaning back in his chair. "Well, it's not going to work, Swift. I'm going to treat you with kid gloves. My people will move you to a federal prison, you'll get a fair trial, and then you'll rot in the pen for the rest of your life."

Kennedy shoved himself back from the desk, pointing toward the cell. "Get in there, Swift. I have to finish your travel plans. You're going in style, kid. I've got an armored personnel carrier coming for you from a nearby army base."

He ordered Tom to stand in the far corner of the cell, then slammed the barred door shut. "Hope you're not too uncomfortable, Swift. When you leave here, we'll give you a pair of shoes. Until then, what you're wearing is what you've got. I'm not allowing you to have even a mattress or a blanket in there. Who know what you could get up to with a few bedsprings and a blanket?"

Kennedy heaved the square isotope carrying case beside the desk lamp.

"Thought you'd enjoy getting a long last

look at this, Swift. You'll never see it again. Evidence, you know."

The federal agent whistled, and a sheriff's deputy straightened up beside the office gun rack. Kennedy pointed to the uncomfortable stool Tom had just vacated. "I want you to sit here and keep an eye on this punk at all times."

Now Kennedy stopped by the gun rack, coming back with a riot shotgun and a box of ammunition. He pumped the gun, working shells into it.

"If the kid tries anything funny—even if he just wiggles his ears—waste him."

Stepping outside, Kennedy paused for a second, giving Tom a grin. "You have yourself a nice rest, Swift. I know you must be tired after all the running around you've been doing. I'll be back for you in a little while."

Tom sat on a splintery wooden bench chained to the cell wall, staring glumly through the bars. Across from him but well out of reach was the deputy, the shotgun across his knees. The guy was big and brawny, with the beginnings of a gut straining the buttons on his khaki shirt. His features were set in a frown, and eyes like a pair of BBs bored relentlessly into Tom.

Finally, Tom couldn't stand looking at the guy anymore and shifted his gaze to the desk.

His small movement brought the deputy bolt upright on the stool, shotgun ready.

Tom ignored the deputy, staring bleakly at the isotope case on the desk. There was his ticket out of this madhouse of a universe. He had to get back home—he *had* to. With every passing second, Tom's chances of getting back got worse and worse. What was going on in his home universe? Judging by Thomas Swift's past record, he was a dangerous man to have in any world. What was he doing now with Tom's mom and dad, with Sandra—with Rick, Dan, and Mandy?

Tom's thoughts were interrupted when the door to the sheriff's office banged open. A girl had knocked it with her hips and come in carrying a covered tray. She was dressed in a tight, slightly stained waitress uniform and looked completely bored as she popped her gum.

It took Tom a moment to recognize this vision as Mandy Coster.

"Hey, fella," she said to the deputy. "I just come over from the cafe with dinner for the prisoner."

"Haven't seen you before," the lawman said in a raspy voice.

"Just started today." Mandy glanced over at Tom. "So what's the deal? You want me to show you what's in here so you'll know we ain't smuggling a hacksaw in the meatloaf?"

She held out the tray, whipped off the cover—and a bristling, furious alley cat leaped for the guard's grinning face. Raising one hand to protect his eyes from the yowling attacker, the deputy swung his shotgun toward Mandy.

She batted the barrels away with her tray, then smashed it into the guy's face. The deputy reeled, stumbling against the bars of Tom's cell. He was still trying to get his gun aimed at Mandy.

But now Tom was able to get into the fight. He snatched the shotgun's stock, forcing the barrels down. The deputy triggered one blast into the floor. Mandy was still whacking away. At last the man toppled, unconscious, while the cat, spitting and yowling, jumped out one of the barred windows.

Working quickly, Mandy handcuffed the deputy, took his keys, and unlocked Tom's cell. He darted for the door, but she held his arm, counting down on her wristwatch.

"Three, two, one . . . Okay!"

From out in the street, Tom heard the sounds of a battalion-size firefight.

"Where did you get the reinforcements?" he asked.

"You'll see in a minute." Mandy led him out the front door of the office, down the block, and around the corner. They were moving away from the sound of the gunfire. Tom noticed lots of people, many of them armed, heading toward the noise. Nobody paid any attention to Tom and Mandy. They rounded another corner, and there was the Cord.

Mandy urged him inside. "Keep down," she ordered, taking off the waitress cap and pulling on a sweater.

"Where did you get that outfit?" Tom asked.

"It wasn't easy. The girl inside didn't want to give it up." She grinned. "I finally had to bop her for it." Then her smile faded. "That was *my* job. I had help for the rest. I'm sure you'll remember them—Dinwiddie and Finn." Her voice sank. "I needed them, Tom."

A moment later, two men came running down the block. Tom recognized both of them from photos in the newsmagazine article on Thomas Swift. The two men piled into the back of the car. "Great to see you, boss," Dinwiddie, big and red-faced, wheezed. He looked as if he expected Tom to hit him. Grinning nervously, he showed his hands, covered with scratches. "I'm the one who caught the cat."

Finn's greasy dark hair was plastered to his face with sweat. "We were in the hideout in the mountains when we heard you were still around. We tried to find you—"

Tom realized that the intense little man was terrified of him, too.

"And almost did at that motel. Then we heard they'd caught you. Figuring this was the easiest place to spring you, we came to try and found this girl in your Cord." Finn looked as if he weren't sure how Tom would react.

"Yeah," Dinwiddie said with a grin. "Pretty nice, boss." He turned bright red and hurried on. "She had a good plan, too. Sent Finn to buy two gross of firecrackers. Then we wound up scattering them all over the north side of town."

"This is some surprise," Tom said honestly, wondering what else to say. "You pulled it off nice and slick. Thanks, guys."

Mandy, her eyes shining, squeezed Tom's hand. "You didn't think we were going to let some lousy cops lock up our boss, did you?" she joked. "So where do we go now?"

Her eyes faltered when she saw the grim expression on Tom's face. "There's only one place to go—right back to where it all started. I've got to get back to that shack in the hills over White Sand Valley."

"But you can't!" Finn protested. "The cops know about that hideout now. They're sure to come looking for you."

"I know that, I know." Tom gave the man a fierce look, and Finn sank into scared silence.

Lowering his voice, Tom whispered to Mandy.

"It's the only place on this earth where I can get home." *If* I can get home, he thought grimly.

15

THOMAS SWIFT PUT DOWN HIS ELECTRIC welder with a satisfied smile. "There," he said. "That's the last adjustment to the containment field generator. I feel a little self-conscious. I've never really had an audience while committing a crime."

He glanced over at the small group sitting behind the now-open blast shields. They might be an audience, but there was no chance that they'd applaud what he was doing.

Five people were arranged in a row of chairs: Tom Swift, Sr., Mrs. Swift, Sandra, Mandy, and Rick. Each person had his or her hands tied to the arms of the chairs, and all of them were gagged.

"Sorry about the ropes," Thomas said. "I

kind of need them, though. They'll disappear soon enough, after the, uh ... accident."

Thomas Swift smiled thinly. "It'll be an awful tragedy. All the people close to Tom Swift, taken in one big boom. In a way, it's like what happened in my world, when I was a little kid. You should be proud of your son, Mr. Swift. He actually did pierce the veil between universes with his black hole thing. Of course, I think my space-warp experiment on the other side may have had something to do with it. You see," he explained, "I'm a hunted criminal in my world, and I created this gizmo to escape."

Sitting down at the control panel, Thomas went on. "There's a lot more I can do in this world, especially with Swift Enterprises behind me. Look at it this way, Dad. If I play my cards right, your grandson might be the emperor of the world."

The look in Tom senior's eyes said that Thomas was no son of his. But he looked in amazement at how well this stranger had mastered the equipment for Tom's experiment.

Rick heard a familiar bass hum throbbing through him as the containment field came into existence. Then came the shrieking cry of the lasers powering up. The robot arm swung the fusion fuel into the target area.

The lasers fired, and Thomas Swift cut in

the particle accelerator. The streams of energy blazed together as before, blindingly bright. Then the tiny ball of painful, dark blue light appeared, sucking in the energy.

Thomas Swift smiled. Everything was going according to plan. This uncanny glow had to be the dark light Cantwell had told him about.

He started manipulating his controls. Now to use the field to shift the black hole toward his intended victims . . .

A universe away, Tom Swift worked frantically over the ruined equipment he'd found in the shack. Although the forces of law and order had probably found the wreckage, they'd been too busy chasing him to cart it away.

Also, Tom had to admit, although Thomas Swift's apparatus was crude, it was sturdy. The solid gold buss bars hadn't melted when the power blew through them, although some of the hand-wired circuits had. All the vacuum tubes had shattered as well. Tom had foreseen that and had already purchased replacements.

Even the melted wiring wasn't so bad. If Tom had had to replace a printed circuit, he'd have been completely out of luck, and he had a complete map of the way everything had been built in Thomas Swift's computer.

Tom's first order of business had been to

move the equipment down toward the valley. Dinwiddie, Finn, and Mandy had been recruited as reluctant laborers for that job.

"Why are we doing this?" Dinwiddie grumbled as he and Finn lugged the heavy buss bar to the new work site.

"Part of my new plan," Tom said out loud. More quietly, he whispered to Mandy, "I've been wondering why the black hole moved in my first experiment. I think it was because of the experiment that Thomas Swift was running here. We sort of met each other halfway, creating a tunnel between universes."

Tom frowned. "The problem was, our portals weren't in exactly the same place. Each exerted a pull on the other, so they drifted." He glanced worriedly at his watch. So much time had passed. Could he reopen the tunnel to his home universe? Or had that pathway already healed over?

"Put it down right there, guys." He pointed to the growing pile of equipment on the valley floor. "If my calculations are correct," he muttered to Mandy, "that's the exact location of the testing bunker in my world. I want to get as close as possible in space. Because when Thomas Swift creates another black hole—and I'm sure he will somehow—I want our connection to be as stable as possible."

Mandy shook her head in confusion. "I'm

just glad we're moving this sucker downhill, instead of up."

As evening came on, they had not only moved the equipment but had just about restored it. Mandy turned out to be deft at replacing vacuum tubes, and Finn turned out to be the guy who'd originally wired the circuits they were now repairing. Tom spent his time testing and comparing the finished products to Thomas Swift's plans.

He worked particularly on the containment field, where the radioactive isotopes were bombarded with high-energy lasers. If that failed, he and most of California would be spread over the earth's surface.

Finally, he carefully set the nuclear fuel rods in their positions. Then he slipped into the heavy biker's leathers he'd bought for his second journey between universes.

"Well," Tom said, zipping himself in, "I guess this is it."

Mandy grabbed his hand. "You know, Swift, I'm gonna miss you. Before you came along, I was letting that cruddy cousin of mine call the shots. You sure managed to shake up my life."

Tom looked at her for a long moment. "I'm sorry about what happened."

"Don't be. Dan's history—or will be, after I pry a few bucks loose from the million he got for ratting on you. Then I'm going back to school." Tears appeared in Mandy's eyes. "You're a special guy, Tom, and you gave me a special gift. You let me know I can be better than I am, and I promise you, I'm not going to blow it."

Thomas Swift's henchmen were waiting to say goodbye as well. "You gonna try that experiment again?" Dinwiddie asked.

"This time, maybe I'll get it right." He faced the two. "Okay. Mandy will drive you out of here. She gets the Cord, and I want you to treat her right. I hear anything else, and I'll be coming after you. Understand?"

It was pure bluff, but he'd read Finn and Dinwiddie perfectly. They went pale and nodded mutely.

While the two got in the car, Tom whispered to Mandy, "You also get the computer, and whatever money is left." He grinned. "Think about paying that poor motel owner for the cabin we burned down."

Mandy grabbed a quick kiss and ran for the Cord. "Now get out of here before the cops finally close in," Tom called after them.

Minutes after the Cord had disappeared into the hills, a rocket flashed over the rim of the valley. It made a direct hit on the old shack, blowing it to bits.

"Looks like Agent Kennedy has started playing hardball," Tom muttered, feeding power to the warp portal.

Thomas Swift's containment field was much stronger than the one Tom had designed. It left a wavering pattern in the air like a heat shimmer. Inside, the lasers cycled up, feeding short bursts of intense energy to the nuclear fuel rods.

Now the field contracted, becoming like a shadow. The fuel rods were forced together, and the reaction took place. There should have been a catastrophic explosion, but the field held, pushing the force back upon itself and forcing a rift in the very fabric of the universe.

Tom saw the now-familiar blue glow beginning to form.

On the hillsides, he heard the shouts and shots of hundreds of law officers swarming down toward him. Above, he heard the ominous *thwip-thwip-thwip* of Kennedy's helicopter coming in for the kill.

Still, Tom stood frozen in front of his controls. He wanted to make sure Kennedy's task force kept its attention on him, rather than chasing Mandy. Tom also had to admit that the prospect of reentering the mad world of the Negative Zone scared him stiff.

They were closing in. Everyone had seen him now. Tom wondered what Kennedy would make of his disappearing act.

But then, with luck, another Tom Swift might come tumbling back into this universe.

Tom could only hope.

Forcing himself to be calm, he stared through the containment field at the disturbing blue globe. Now the glow was outshining the dimming effects of the field. The field itself was breaking up, warped out of existence.

The eye-tearing ball of nonlight was almost a yard wide. It glowed balefully. The police officers, government agents, and troops closing in hesitated uneasily. Tom could understand their fear.

"What are you waiting for?" Kennedy's voice boomed from the helicopter.

Tom glanced up to see the federal agent bracing himself in the cockpit, trying to draw a bead on him with his .44 Magnum.

This is it, Tom thought.

Drawing a deep breath, Tom flung himself forward into the blue glow—into the event horizon of the black hole.

16

THE NEGATIVE ZONE WAS AS STRANGE, twisted, and terrifying to Tom as it had been before. But this time he was ready. The shock of transition didn't knock him unconscious as he went pinwheeling through the sickly non-light of the zone. He paid no attention to the bizarre sights around him, watching for only one thing—the light at the end of the tunnel.

When the pinhole of real light appeared, Tom aimed toward it. Either this was the entrance to his universe, or . . . The alternative didn't bear thinking about.

The light was near, now. Tom braced himself. An instant later, he was tumbling into the experiment vault of the testing bunker.

He was shocked but conscious! And his heavy leather suit had survived the stresses of passing through the Negative Zone. Tom was glad he was heavily dressed. A strong breeze battered against him as he forced himself away from the blue glow.

Tom knew where the breeze was coming from—the blast shields had been opened. He fought his way against the gale, then froze as he saw the scene through the open shields. His parents, Sandra, Rick, and Mandy! Thomas Swift had placed them right in the path of destruction of the black hole!

His parents and friends stared in silent amazement at Tom's sudden appearance. They couldn't give him away, though, gagged as they were.

"Stupid machine! Why aren't you working?"

That voice—it was Tom's own! Tom launched himself for the opening. Sitting at a control panel, frantically hitting switches, was his evil twin. Thomas Swift was identical. He was even wearing Tom's favorite T-shirt.

"Why isn't the black hole moving?" Thomas Swift cried in frustration. "The containment field is working properly, and it can't budge this stupid thing. But Cantwell said the hole moved!"

"That's because your hole was located up on the hillside, not down here," Tom said.

Thomas Swift whirled in his chair, but Tom was already leaping for him.

The chair went over with a crash as they grappled. Thomas Swift was staring up in shock, but then he began fighting viciously. He tried to butt Tom with his head, to break Tom's nose.

When Tom pulled back, Thomas wriggled like a snake to get free. The second he was up, Thomas Swift grabbed a chair, smashing it down on his rival.

I should have realized this guy would fight dirty, Tom thought sourly as he desperately dodged Thomas's follow-through kick. He swept his legs to catch his evil twin behind the knees, sending Thomas Swift toppling to the floor.

They rolled around on the floor like a couple of scrapping boys, but they were perfectly matched. Each time one seemed to gain the upper hand, the other escaped, evaded, or launched a counterblow.

Tom didn't know how long the fight went on before it was interrupted by a muffled moan from one of the prisoners. Thomas Swift glanced at Mandy in irritation, then froze in midpunch as he stared over her shoulder.

Wary of a trick, Tom snatched only a quick peek. But he froze and stared, too, when he saw the problem. Almost half of the experiment vault was now filled with a glowing blue halo.

"The black hole—it's getting stronger. Got to shut it off!" Tom tore open the emergency power controls. But when he hit the switches, they were as useless as they'd been the last time.

"Didn't you install new cutoffs? That was our problem the last time!"

Thomas Swift's face was pale, but his expression was nasty. "I didn't *know* I had to do that. Your stupid friend Cantwell didn't mention the problem."

"You mean, you didn't ask. You just saw this as the perfect accident." Tom went to the equipment closet and came back with a sledgehammer and a mallet. "I expect that at least you know where the cable guillotines are. We'll have to go in and hit them manually."

Thomas Swift nodded, reaching for the sledgehammer. Tom jerked it back. "I'm not a fool, you know. I'm keeping the better weapon." He shoved the mallet into his alter ego's hand and let him lead the way into the vault.

The wind was reaching hurricane force now, and the glow made it difficult to see. "Take the one on the near wall," Tom yelled over the bellowing rush of air.

As he plunged on into the room, he heard a new and more ominous sound—a creaking from the ceiling above. It was made of three feet of reinforced concrete, with ten feet of dirt on top, but it was feeling the strain of the hungry black hole below it. If they didn't cut this thing off, and quick, the whole bunker could fall down around their ears.

Tom was just edging past the blue glow when he felt a hand between his shoulders. "So long, sucker," Thomas Swift hissed in his ear. "I can take care of this myself."

He hooked one of Tom's ankles and shoved viciously, trying to trip him, to send him into the event horizon of the black hole. The world turned blue as the hole sucked greedily for him.

Tom swung his sledgehammer, not to hit Thomas, but in a frantic attempt to anchor himself. The heavy head caught between two cable brackets, and Tom's fall was broken. He clung to the handle, fighting desperately against the relentless pull.

He was already on the threshold of the Negative Zone. His arms seemed abnormally long, as if they'd been stretched while they gripped the sledgehammer handle. Time seemed to move strangely, too. It felt like an eternity as Tom managed to work his way back, hand over hand, toward normal reality.

Tom knew he had to move quickly. The black hole was growing. As the glow of non-light expanded, he'd be deeper and deeper in the zone.

Thomas Swift knew that, too. He had

grabbed on to a stanchion and was kicking at Tom's hammer, trying to dislodge it, or even better, to knock it from Tom's hands.

He was beginning to look distorted, too, one leg stretching far too long in a crazy perspective. Thomas Swift's body seemed miles off, but his foot appeared enormous as it flew at Tom. It was taking on the unearthly geometry of the Negative Zone.

Tom knew he had only one chance. As the foot crashed down on him, he shifted his grasp from the hammer handle to Thomas Swift's ankle.

A wild, terrified cry burst from Tom's alter ego as he felt the sucking pressure on him suddenly doubled. He frenziedly tried to pull himself out of the blue glow with his arms while kicking at Tom with his free leg. Tom ignored the attempts to peel him off and concentrated on trying to get farther from the black hole. Then, up ahead, he saw exactly what he needed—a heavy piece of equipment bolted to the floor, with a nice, heavy metal handle set in its side.

With a final tug on Thomas Swift's leg, Tom managed to grab the ring. But that extra bit of pressure was just too much for his evil twin. Shrieking, Thomas Swift lost his grip on the stanchion. His hands flailed as he sought something, anything to cling to.

There was nothing in reach.

He whipped past Tom, his face distorted by terror. Then, as he fell deeper into the negative zone, he became even more twisted by the strange geometry. Tom's last sight of Thomas Swift was much like his first one, when they had passed in the negative zone. His twin looked misshapen, grotesque, yet horribly familiar.

As Thomas disappeared, Tom felt a momentary lessening of the unbearable pull on him, almost as if the black hole had its mouth full. He took immediate advantage, throwing himself farther from the event horizon, closer to the normal world.

It was still an awful struggle, getting loose from that terrible grip. Tom's entire body was beaded with sweat when he finally got free, but he was able to move. He found the mallet that Thomas Swift had left behind and staggered to the power guillotine set in the wall.

The antilight glow was perilously close now. It was almost filling the vault. Tom reached the cutoff and swung. There was an explosion of energy, a brilliant discharge of sheer power, but the line was cut. The room filled with the stink of ozone as the blue glow suddenly deformed.

Tom dashed to the other cutoff and swung blindly, averting his face from a second blast.

The lasers were off now. Tom stared fearfully at the darklight glow. Had the black hole grown large enough to sustain itself? If it had, cutting the power wouldn't kill it, and slowly but surely, it would eat the planet Earth alive.

Now the glow seemed to be shrinking. Tom turned from the experiment vault back to the people trapped in the observation room. He tore at the bonds keeping Mandy in her chair, and together they freed Rick and Tom's family.

Mr. and Mrs. Swift and Sandra were still wobbly from whatever drug Thomas had given them and needed help to get to the stairs.

"Hey!" Rick said as he trailed along behind them. "The glow—it's gone!"

Tom froze on the stairs, peering back. "Are you sure?"

"Not a trace of it. No wind, no glow, no nothing. Want me to check inside?"

"No!" Tom yelled.

Before Rick could head back toward the equipment, the concrete roof of the experiment vault gave a long, groaning sound. Cracks suddenly appeared in the walls. As Tom and the others frantically made their way up the stairs, the roof of the vault, and then the observation room, collapsed with a roar.

Tom, his family, and his friends stood silently looking at the bunker—or rather, the hole in the ground where the bunker had been.

"Looks like you've lost your equipment again," Tom's father finally said.

"And as far as I'm concerned, it can stay buried." Tom shook his head. "No way do I want to open a gate to this universe for another Thomas Swift."

The collapse of the bunker had not gone unnoticed. From the distance, they heard the wail of sirens approaching. Tom breathed a long sigh of relief. Once again, sirens meant that help was on the way, not that he'd have to fear arrest.

Harlan Ames arrived with the first wave of rescue workers. He stared in disbelief when he heard Mr. Swift's story.

"We came through all right," Tom's father said, ending the story, "thanks to Tom—the real Tom—here."

"I still think we should take you, Mrs. Swift, and Sandra to the hospital to check for any aftereffects," Ames said.

Mr. Swift nodded tiredly.

"What about the testing bunker?" Ames continued.

"Make sure all power is cut to that equipment, then bulldoze it." Mr. Swift's face was grim as Ames helped him, with the rest of his family, to an ambulance. "We can build a new testing vault."

Tom, Rick, and Mandy followed the ambulance to the hospital. "They seem fine, if a little worn out," the nurse at the emergency room said. "This is really just a formality."

Relieved, Tom sat down with Rick and Mandy to swap stories. His friends brought Tom up-to-date on the activities of his evil twin. Then Tom revealed some of his adventures in the alternate universe.

"So I was a hick-town cop, and Mandy helped you escape," Rick said. "But we were the same, right? Identical?"

"Well, you looked pretty much the same, but you didn't act the same." Tom glanced at Mandy and felt his face getting warm.

She gave him a piercing glance. "What do you mean?"

"Well, let's just say the Mandy in that universe kissed a lot differently."

"Oh, yeah?" Mandy inquired, her hands on her hips. "And how scientifically did you test that out?"

"I wouldn't say it was a question of science," Tom protested.

"I would," Mandy said. "I thought that was the whole idea—experiments that could be duplicated in other laboratories." She gave Tom a look. "Why don't you pick me up later? Maybe we can discuss a course of research."

Tom grinned. "Now, that's an experiment I'd love to try."

Tom's next adventure:

Tom Swift's latest invention may revolutionize sports technology. His ingenious computer-controlled exoskeleton pumps and primes every muscle to the max. And now it has transformed Tom's friend Rick Cantwell into a contender for the kickboxing championship of the world!

But with the thrill of power comes a jolt of terror. For while the energy disks harden the muscles, they also warp the mind—with dangerous results. When an unscrupulous kickboxer threatens to exploit the device, Tom's only chance to stop him is to don the high-risk, high-tech armor himself . . . in Tom Swift #3, *Cyborg Kickboxer*.

ENTER THE TOM SWIFT SWEEPSTAKES!
1 GRAND PRIZE: Macintosh® Classic®
Personal Computer
10 FIRST PRIZES: BMX RANDOR BICYCLE

**Entry limited to 17 years of age and under.
All entries must be received by 5/1/91.**

Official Sweepstakes Rules

NO PURCHASE NECESSARY. To enter, fill out entry form available at participating retailers during the promotional period; or fill out entry form in the back of <u>The Black Dragon</u> and <u>The Negative Zone</u>, Archway Paperbacks' books published by Pocket Books, available at participating retailers during the promotional period; or hand print your name, address, zip code, age and phone number on a post card and mail it to:

TOM SWIFT SWEEPSTAKES, Archway Paperbacks, Dept. TSS
1230 Avenue of the Americas, New York, NY 10020

Enter as often as you wish. Each entry form must be mailed separately. Entrants must be 17 years of age and under. All entries must be received by May 1, 1991. Photocopies or other mechanical reproductions of completed entries will not be accepted. Simon & Schuster, Inc. is not responsible for lost, misdirected or late mail.

All winners will be selected at random. All interpretations of the rules and decisions by Simon & Schuster, Inc. are final. All winners will be selected from among entries received by May 1, 1991. Drawing will be held on or about May 15, 1991. Winners will be notified by telephone or mail. Odds of winning will be determined by the total number of entries received.

The estimated value of the Grand Prize, an Apple Macintosh® Classic® personal computer, including monitor, keyboard, mouse, and system software, is $999.00. There are ten first prizes and the estimated retail price per first prize of a BMX Randor Boys bike is $90.00. Arrangements for the grand prize and first prize fulfillment to be made by Simon & Schuster, Inc.

Prizes are nontransferable. Taxes on all prizes awarded will be the sole responsibility of the winners. Simon & Schuster, Inc. reserves the right to substitute prizes of a value approximately comparable to that exhibited in the promotional campaign, or the cash equivalent to Simon & Schuster, Inc's estimated retail value of obtaining the prize, if for any reason Simon & Schuster, Inc. is unable to furnish the specific items described.

Sweepstakes open to citizens and residents of the United States and Canada, 17 years of age and under, except employees and their families of Apple Computer. Inc., Simon & Schuster, Inc., affiliated companies, subsidiaries, advertising and promotional agencies and participating retailers. Void where prohibited by law.

In order to win a prize, residents of Canada will be required to correctly answer a skill question administered by mail. Any litigation respecting the conduct and awarding of a prize in this publicity contest by a resident of the province of Quebec may be submitted to the regie des loteries et courses du Quebec.

Each prize winner and/or his/her parent or legal guardian will be required to sign and return an Affidavit of Eligibility and compliance with official rules, within thirty (30) days of notification attempt. Noncompliance within this time period will result in disqualification and an alternate winner will be selected. Grand prize winner may be requested to consent to use of name and likeness for publicity and advertising.

For a list of Sweepstakes winners (available August 15, 1991), send a self-addressed, stamped envelope to:

TOM SWIFT WINNERS, Archway Paperbacks, Dept. TSW
1230 Avenue of the Americas, New York, NY 10020

Tom Swift is a registered trademark of Simon & Schuster, Inc.
©1990 Apple Computer, Inc. Apple, the Apple logo, Macintosh are registered trademarks of Apple Computer, Inc. Classic is a registered trademark licensed to Apple Computer Inc.

 **Archway Paperbacks**
Published by Pocket Books

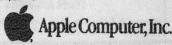 Apple Computer, Inc.

OFFICIAL ENTRY FORM

Name_____

Address_____

City_____State_____Zip Code_____

Phone_____Age_____

239